Forests of the
Night

MARGARET MOORE

Forests of the Night

Walker and Company
New York

Published in the United States of America in 1988 by the
Walker Publishing Company, Inc.

Library of Congress Cataloging-in-Publication Data

Moore, Margaret.
    Forests of the night.

    I. Title.
PR6063.0619F67 1988   823'.914   87-37265
ISBN 0-8027-5707-3

Printed in the United States of America

10 9 8 7 6 5 4 3 2 1

Tiger, tiger, burning bright
In the forests of the night

William Blake
The Tiger

CHAPTER 1

A red mark on a white sheet. Not a pretty way to think about a woman, Luke Mason told himself, shoving the list of names into the hip pocket of his jeans before ringing the doorbell. Not the way he'd have thought about anybody at the start of his fieldwork placement in Holtchester. But ironically enough it was exactly how his supervisor and her kind expected the young Left to think. One month of child guidance and he was conforming to stereotype. Almost dehumanized.

But not quite, he realized, as Cheryl Hobbs opened the door of her council house a few minutes after noon that October Thursday. She kept a firm grip on the latch but there was no mistaking the challenge in those cool grey eyes. Luke did homage to the uplifted curves of left arm and breast, the flat belly and long legs beneath faded grey cords.

'Well?' Cheryl's glance travelled over his shoulder towards the houses opposite.

'Mrs Hobbs?' He recalled the name with difficulty. 'I'm from the child guidance clinic. Luke Mason—social worker.'

'Oh?' Cheryl threw back her dark head, making little effort to mask her distaste. 'You're new?'

'Temporary assignment. Tomorrow's my last day, in fact. Mrs Tomlinson asked me to call.'

'Can't imagine why. Martin's off the books now. Dr Denny said last June he needn't go back.'

'I know. This is by way of a routine follow-up. To make sure things are going smoothly. To ask if the clinic can be of any further help.'

Cheryl laughed. The harsh sound grated, but why should it? Unattached women needed tough carapaces, if they were bringing up children on council estates. Anna, Luke's girlfriend—his ex-girlfriend?—had told him all about that, in the days and nights when they had time to spare for each other. As the cold Fenland mist condensed into drizzle, he mourned for the irretrievable.

'Mrs T doesn't give up without a struggle, does she?'

Luke grunted, aborting a disloyal grin. Tomorrow Hilde would be writing up her final assessment of his performance for the benefit of his Polytechnic tutors. If he hadn't been her ideal casework trainee he had at least striven to keep his nose clean. One false move today and she could still fail him. At worst that could mean ejection from the postgraduate social work course he'd sweated blood to get on to. At best a second compulsory placement in a child guidance setting.

'No thanks,' Cheryl said crisply. 'I don't think you can be of any help to us. Unless you happen to be good with typewriters.'

'*Typewriters?*' Whatever Luke had expected it wasn't this. Sounded like some crazy mental flexibility test. For half a second he wondered if his supervisor had put her up to it. Then he rallied. This was what his brand of social work was about. Responding to clients' real needs, not the needs your theories told you they ought to have.

'Well,' he said, 'I've used a portable for a couple of years and I'm fairly mechanically minded . . .'

'Come in then, if you like, and see if you can get any action out of my machine. It seized up an hour ago and there's a job I must finish today.'

Her living-room surprised him slightly. Among the mass-produced pine and teak veneer there was a sprinkling of Victoriana—a workbox, a tea-table, a landscape in oils. The typewriter, an oldish electric model, stood on the dining-table. Luke checked the connections, re-wired the plug, changed the fuse and administered a few prods to the interior. Without effect.

'No joy?'

He shook his head, accepting the proffered cigarette.

'Beyond my ken. We'd better get it to a repair shop.' Hilde would have pounced on that 'we'. Over-involvement with the client was a major crime in her book.

'They don't service this make in Holtchester. And the Cambridge shop closes on Thursdays—like ours. That's why you found me at home. But you know my habits, I dare say. You'll have read the notes.'

She perched, legs crossed, on the arm of the settee, scratching an invisible irritant on one of her sandalled feet. Her small breasts hung loose beneath a white T-shirt.

He laughed.

'I'm not much of a reader. You work in a bookshop, don't you? By the looks of things, you're a glutton for work.' He gestured to the sheets of handwritten copy. 'Why not borrow your office typewriter?'

'This is it. The Poulencs let me keep it at home. It's a small business and there isn't much typing. I do it here and get time off in lieu. Usually there's nothing urgent, but this is. Price list for their stall at the first book fair of the university term.'

Luke stood up, feeling useless.

'Sorry.'

'Never mind. Don't expect much from your lot.'

And why should she? He had a vision of Cheryl, slumped on a plastic chair in the clinic waiting-room, riffling through a dog-eared colour supplement. And ranged against her the paraphernalia of authority—the filing cabinets, the small telephone switchboard, the appointments diary. And the disapproving stare of their guardian, the secretary-receptionist, as she interrupted her typing to monitor the behaviour of unaccompanied children. *Typing* . . .

'The clinic runs to a typewriter of sorts. I use it myself now and then. Any good? It would be available after six.'

Cheryl giggled, uncrossing these long, delicious legs. Her earrings glinted briefly.

'Do you think Mrs T would approve?'

'No reason for her to know. She'll be on leave till tomorrow.'

'OK, you're on. You'll be there to let me in?'

Luke nodded. Holtchester owed him. And an evening with Cheryl Hobbs might go part way to repaying the debt.

'Sevenish would suit me best. Martin will be up at Browne —at the youth club.'

'Settled down, has he?' Luke needed data for his written record of the visit. 'No more problems at school?' He tried to crystallize his hazy recollections of the reasons for the boy's referral to child guidance.

'No—no. Everything's been fine since he started at Browne.' Hilde would observe that the lady had protested too much, but she was welcome to her suspicions. 'It was the last class teacher he had in the primary school that got up his nose,' Cheryl added as an unsolicited bonus.

'Yes?' Hating himself, Luke administered the standard prompt for amplification. But his informant evidently knew the tricks of the trade at least as well as he. Her face stiffened.

'Past history, isn't it? God, I'd forgotten the time. Kid'll be home for his lunch in a minute.'

'I'll be off. See you around seven?'

'Lovely.'

Rain streamed down the windscreen as he mounted his motorbike. He retrieved the caselist from his pocket and crossed out Cheryl's name. Then he scribbled brief notes of the visit for the clinic file and his fieldwork diary. Not a word about the typewriter business, of course. Perfectly legit but irrelevant to the case. A case that was closed, as far as Cheryl and he were concerned.

Nothing wrong with a friendly gesture to an ex-client, was there? Even if that client looked like a girl who knew how to repay kindly gestures when she was in the mood. And Luke would certainly be in need of tender loving care after three or four hours' hard work polishing up that field diary with tomorrow's grilling from his supervisor in prospect. As he rode out of the drab estate and through the bustle of the town centre he imagined the sweet-salt taste of Cheryl's skin, the provocation of her brown fingers.

It was just on 12.25, well before rush hour, when he reached the bar counter of the Blue Waggon, his habitual refuge from working lunches at the clinic.

'Have it on me.' The light Edinburgh voice took him by surprise. He swivelled round to confront the pink, round face of Jane Gordon.

'Glad I ran into you, Luke. Can't make the farewell booze-up tomorrow.' Friday, he remembered, was Jane's full research day. She worked six half-day sessions as an educational psychologist, but most of that time was spent in schools. Her path crossed with Luke's only on Tuesdays when the full clinic team met for the joint diagnosis of new cases and conferences on ongoing treatment.

'How will it feel to be off the hook?'

Luke imagined himself as a salmon gasping at the end of Jane's line, as she arranged plates and cutlery on a small table.

'Little chance of that with thirteen months' training ahead of me. But it'll feel good to be done with therapy. And I can pick optional subjects to suit the branch of the trade I want to practise—community social work.'

'As an end or the means to an end?'

He shrugged. 'Time will tell.' The interrogation bugged him, and it was showing. Women like Jane Gordon were apt to view Marxism as something nasty in other people's woodsheds.

'Sorry, Luke. Shouldn't have asked. Psychological testing's getting into my blood, I'm afraid.'

'Then why do it?' Not for the money, he deduced, costing her flame Viyella blouse and matching cashmere cardigan, and recalling that her husband was a Reader at Cambridge University.

'I like to fund my own research expenses. Besides, the contacts I'm making in schools could come in handy for future projects.'

One or two standard prompts and Jane was rabbiting on about her current inquiry into computer based maths teaching. Luke munched the chicken sandwiches he couldn't have afforded to buy and elaborated his fantasies of the evening ahead. It was a good five minutes before she detected his lack of involvement.

'Boring you stiff, I daresay. Usually keep mum about research when I'm in the clinic. Not really compatible with human resources therapy, is it?'

'Few other human activities are—or so I gather from Hilde Tomlinson.'

Jane giggled, metamorphosing into the Naughty Girl of the Lower Fourth. 'I'm glad our Hilde hasn't brainwashed you. She tries hard enough, God knows. Which reminds me —she made me promise to confer with you on someone or other this week. I quite forgot yesterday. Now who the hell . . .?' She unearthed a notebook from her vast bucket bag. 'Ah yes, it was the Hobbs child.'

Luke observed with some surprise her heightened colour and slight grimace. She had not struck him as a woman who was easily embarrassed.

'Have you seen the mother?' she asked.

'Briefly.'

'Everything OK?'

'Everything except her typewriter.' No harm in Jane knowing. She wouldn't be seeing Hilde before she wrote up his assessment. And there was little danger of her charging over from her home in Newnham to spoil the party. She laughed at his account of his modest initiative.

'Sounds as though Hilde must accept the fact that the case is well and truly closed. She asked me to make inquiries about the boy when I was in his school this week. So I had a word with his year counsellor and John Henderson, the

Acting Head. Henderson's very keen on pastoral care. You'll have heard of him?'

'Vaguely.' Jane's discomfort seemed to be evaporating.

'Impressive character. He's had a lot to do with Browne's track record. Their attendance figures and exam results are way above average for local comprehensives. And they cope well with disturbed and difficult kids.'

'A shining example of human resources therapy?'

'Anything but.' Jane laughed again. She was an easier companion than he had anticipated. 'No, Browne's steered clear of the clinic net. Some collaboration is inevitable, of course. Child guidance professionals have statutory responsibilities for handicapped children. But the school has managed to resist absorption into the HRT empire. So far.'

'Things could change?'

'That rather depends.'

'Depends on what?'

'On the Headship appointment. They're interviewing the week after next. Last man was ill for almost a year and John Henderson was running the place long before he officially became Acting Head. So policy won't change if he gets the job.'

'Sounds like a strong contender.'

'If Holtchester wasn't so near Cambridge. There are several dons on the Board of Governors. And they may well plump for a candidate with a higher degree qualification.'

'Who would leave pastoral care to the HRT experts?'

'Possibly.' The skies had cleared now. Luke blinked in a sudden shaft of sunlight, and drained his beerglass.

'Fascinating stuff, Jane, but I suppose we'd better get back to basics. What did the teachers say about Martin Hobbs?'

'He's fine now, I gather.' Jane sounded as eager as Cheryl had done to skate over the topic. 'There was some hassle at the beginning of term, but that's hardly surprising. Kids with a history of school refusal tend to panic after the long summer break. And it's only his second year at Browne.'

'School refusal was the main problem, was it?'

'Uh-huh. Dug his heels in a couple of years ago. Before my time here.'

'Why?'

Jane shrugged her broad shoulders. 'Daresay he found the going too tough. The regime in Greenside Primary's fairly formal and they push the high-fliers in their two last years.'

Cheryl Hobbs would have approved, Luke decided. She had struck him as a girl who could push pretty hard herself if she had a mind to.

'Then there was the business with the father.'

'Yes?'

'Come off it, Luke. You must know as much about it as I do if you've read the file.' Gamma minus.

'I've tried. But the NeoFreudian jargon sticks in the gullet, don't you find?

'Mmm.' Jane caressed her beermug, avoiding eye-contact. 'NeoMarxist jargon is equally unpalatable as far as I'm concerned. But the proverbial grain of salt works wonders.' He was surprised to see how carefully she had manicured her broad hands.

'Bit late in the day for me to try it. And you've such a way with words, Jane. Any chance of a recap?'

'Oh, very well. The details are obscure. But it seems the divorced husband moved back into the area with his new wife and started agitating for access to the boy.'

'And Cheryl refused?' She hadn't come across as a smother-mother. But neither did wild animals till you made a grab for their young.

'She didn't refuse pointblank. Didn't have to. Seems she'd already made such a bogeyman of the father that the boy was a hundred per cent anti.'

'I see. And no doubt there were other father-figures on

the horizon. Cheryl Hobbs struck me as quite a sexy lady.' He hoped it sounded casual.

'And quite a tough lady, to judge by Hilde's notes. She didn't give much away in the casework sessions.'

'But she attended regularly?'

'So it seems. Saw Hilde once a week for the first three or four months of Peter's work with the boy. Traditional team-work approach.'

The two-pronged attack, Luke had once seen it described in the writings of an ex-army child psychiatrist.

'Then what?'

'Then Hilde admitted defeat. The boy continued to see Peter weekly for a year. But the social work sessions with Cheryl were cut down to one a month for the remainder of that year and one every couple of months when Martin was switched to a fortnightly schedule.'

'The other lads at school must have had something to say. Kid must have taken to Peter to have stuck it out for so long.'

'Most kids do. He's a nice bloke, don't you think?'

'Suppose so.' Luke shrugged into his duffel coat. The formal authority invested in the Medical Director was to his mind one of the most obnoxious features of the clinic set-up. But from his limited contacts he judged Peter Denny to be a relatively harmless specimen of a dangerous species.

'Anyhow,' Jane concluded, as she shouldered her bag and stood up, 'Peter and Browne High seem to have done the trick between them. The kid's coping.'

Coping. A bleak word, Luke thought, as he followed her out through the filling bar. The word of an overanxious middle-class mum. But Jane, to the best of his knowledge, was childless.

They said goodbye in the car park. Luke followed Jane's Citroën as far as the T-junction, where she took the right turning for Cambridge and he the left for his bedsit in Wordsworth Square. His route took him past the clinic, a decaying end-terrace house in Disraeli Gardens, an avenue temporarily enlivened by the vivid foliage of its sycamores. The secretary-receptionist, a plump blonde, was locking her pushbike to the railings as he rode by. A bearded face, peering between the lifted curtains of the playroom, reminded him that Thursday was a drama therapy day. He had done well to distance himself from the thumps and screams that would soon be ascending to his temporary office on the first floor.

Eileen Lethbridge pounced on the automatic switchboard in the waiting-room a couple of seconds after it started to ring. Tucking her shorthand version of the message into her blotting-pad, she typed out a fair copy for the Medical Director and opened the door from the waiting-room to his office.

'*Dreadfully* sorry, Doc—Peter.' Five years had failed to obliterate Eileen's liking for courtesy titles. 'No idea you'd still be here, being as it's Thursday. I'd have phoned St Timothy's too, of course, as Mr Pyke said it was urgent. But I know they're not reliable about passing on messages, so I typed the note out for you. Just in case.'

Peter bestowed on her the quick, habitual smile that sweetened his bony face.

'Thanks, Eileen. Glad you did. Shan't be going up to St Tim's this afternoon.' Or any Thursday afternoon. He wondered if she guessed. He'd taken care to leave the office at his usual time, these last six weeks, but there might have been other messages. She wouldn't have wanted to embarrass him by letting him know she knew. Now it didn't matter any more. But he couldn't say anything to her yet. Not before he'd spoken to Cora.

As he dialled the unfamiliar number, his eyes met those of his wife. He picked up the triptych of family photographs. Three fine-boned, handsome faces stared back at him. Faces that claimed their owners' right to be supported in the style to which they had been accustomed. Lance Pyke's voice

crackled over a bad line. One of his clients was getting
stroppy. He'd be tied up until late in Birmingham. Have to
overnight there. Dinner with Peter was out. The prospect of
an empty evening stretched beyond Peter's empty afternoon.
He replaced the receiver. Time. Plenty of time to tell Cora
that the child psychiatry unit at St Timothy's was folding.
And with it the consultancy that covered his children's
boarding-school fees. He'd lost Thursday afternoons six
weeks ago. Last Friday afternoon's session had been his last.
His two Monday sessions would finish at Christmas.

'You'll just have to ask Daddy,' Cora would say, as she
had said before, from behind her *Horse and Hound*. She'd
remind him that he had a talent for begging. And plenty of
experience.

'Oh Christ,' he sobbed drily, covering his face. He
couldn't face her without support. And there was no Hilde
around this afternoon to provide it. From the waiting-room
came the sounds of scuffles and stamping feet. Then Eileen
Lethbridge's voice raised in rebuke. The first members of
the afternoon's drama therapy group had arrived. Time for
him to get out. As he shuffled his papers together, he decided
to make one more 'phone call. But not from his office, where
he might readily be overheard. He was not by nature a
careful man, but he had learnt the hard way to take care of
his professional reputation. Before leaving his room by a
door that led directly into the alley, he checked the locks of
his filing cabinet, cupboard and top lefthand desk drawer.
Once out of the building, he walked quickly to the service
road behind the back gardens of the terrace, where he had
parked his red Maestro.

In the waiting-room Eileen Lethbridge turned her attention to the mail that had arrived by the afternoon post. A
pity Peter Denny had just left—she'd heard the side door
close behind him. She slipped an elastic band round his two
windowed envelopes and stacked the picture postcard for
Luke Mason on top of them. His correspondent's taste

wasn't any better than Luke's if this was typical. Eileen's lip curled at the spectacle of a cruise missile dispersing recognizable fragments of dove. Jane Gordon wouldn't be in until Monday, so her letters could go to the bottom of the pile. The surname had been misspelt as *Gorden* on the envelope that bore the crest of Cambridge University Hospital. And not for the first time—so much for word processors and their scatty young users. Eileen put this stack of mail in her big righthand desk drawer on top of the neatly folded headscarf kept for days when she arrived unprepared for rain.

There was no post for Jos Aiken, the drama therapist. It was a standing joke between them that he could neither read nor write.

'You can't beat the old face-to-face stuff, my love,' he'd tell her with a teasing expression on his broad, ruddy face. Body to body would suit him better, she reckoned. But she never said it right out. Jos's ego was already at bursting point without any help from her.

Hilde Tomlinson's pile of mail was as usual the thickest. Eileen stuffed it into an already bulging folder. Hilde was on leave until tomorrow, officially speaking, but on the basis of past experience, Eileen was prepared to bet she'd be in her office this evening. Catching up on the week's events. Sorting out genuine crises from hardy perennials. Picking up the reins of human resources therapy. So Eileen would take the fat folder of accumulated letters and 'phone messages upstairs in her tea break. Lock it away in a drawer in Hilde's desk to which she held the second key. With all the odd bods that wandered into this place, you couldn't be too careful. Her fingers fiddled with the crucifix she wore over her lacy aquamarine jumper.

'Watch it!' she barked as a bored ten-year-old snatched at his younger companion's Cindy doll. 'None of that nonsense in *my* waiting-room. *If* you please.'

CHAPTER 2

No light showed through the Venetian blinds and insulated curtains of the bay window in the clinic playroom. Good. Just as well not to advertise Cheryl's presence. Luke returned to his Suzuki, parked twenty yards away from the front gate, to await her arrival. It was a quarter past seven when she pedalled round the corner, wearing a blue kagoul as protection against the rain. At his suggestion she left her cycle in the end-of-terrace entry which was screened from Disraeli Gardens by a group of evergreen shrubs. Luke led the way into the building through the side door, which he had left open on its Yale latch, into Peter Denny's office and through the communicating door to the waiting-room.

'Warm enough?' The central heating had been switched off for the night.

'Yes, thanks. I'm pretty tough.' As she pulled off the cape over her head he saw that she had added a fairisle sweater to her tee-shirt, and replaced her sandals with socks and trainers.

'Try it for height.' He patted the typist's chair, realizing that the three or four inches she could have given Eileen Lethbridge were fully accounted for by her long legs.

'It'll do.'

'You smell nice,' he told her as he scrabbled for the drawer key that Eileen kept hidden beneath her blotter. But pricey. He was inhaling the scent of a well-heeled girlfriend of his undergraduate days.

'Joy. Glad you like it. Rather go for it myself, but it's not to everyone's taste.'

A girl who aimed to please, Luke thought, as he opened the righthand drawer of Eileen's desk. Was the perfume chosen for him, and the coppery lip gloss? No sign of either on his lunchtime visit. She didn't budge as his mouth pressed down for a couple of seconds on her cropped, black hair. It might almost have been a boy's head, especially as there were no longer any earrings in the small, pierced ears.

'Better get on with the job, I suppose.' She delved into her rucksack and pulled out a folder.

'OK.'

In his search for the bunch of office keys he unearthed the pile of undistributed correspondence. Beneath it he found the keyring and selected the key for the metal cupboard which housed the typewriter. He carried the shrouded machine over to Cheryl. While she was getting herself organized he read the message on his postcard. Anna and her small daughter were settling down well at the peace camp in the Midlands which they had joined a fortnight earlier. Postage was expensive, so he mustn't expect too many letters. But she'd keep in touch and wished him lots of luck for the new term. No word of her returning to London and no invitations. Ah well, he knew when he wasn't wanted, and when he might be. He returned Cheryl's smile as he replaced the postcard with the other mail in the drawer. A smile cleansed of the resentment so apparent at their earlier meeting.

'How long will this lot take?' He gestured towards the price list.

'An hour maybe. I'm not the world's best typist.'

Luke sat down on one of the vinyl-covered easy chairs ranged around the walls and considered the contents of his briefcase. The field diary was now as good as it was going to be. No point in a further rehash. Better get his teeth into something worthwhile like the paperback edition of *Personal Services and Public Humiliation* he'd promised to review for the winter number of Left Standing. Concentration proved difficult. The chair frame dug into his thighs and the arms inhibited note-taking. After twenty minutes he gave up the effort. Closing his eyes he imagined himself making love to

Cheryl on the pile rug next door in Peter Denny's office. But the irregular bursts of sound generated by the tabulation of author's names, titles, publishers and prices, punctured several promising fantasies well before lift-off. He contemplated with wry amusement the running title of the book on his lap. Tonight's humiliation, if it materialized, would be very, very private.

'So it's your last day tomorrow?' Cheryl's voice roused him. 'Will they give you a big send-off?'

He laughed.

'Hardly. Only been here a month, and I'm not exactly the blue-eyed boy of the establishment. Anyhow, I ought to get back to London soon after lunch. So maybe . . .' Why hadn't he said it sooner? 'Maybe we could celebrate tonight?'

'What did you have in mind?' she asked warily. 'I shouldn't be too late. Martin gets worried. And he'll be home before ten.'

'What about a little drink here? Unless you prefer a quick trip to the local.'

'No thanks. Don't fancy the pubs round here. Holtchester's in the dark ages as far as singles are concerned.'

'OK. I'll nip out for a bottle, if you don't mind being left on your own for a bit.'

'No sweat. I've plenty here to keep me out of mischief. Look. All those bloody little accents to put in by hand.' He saw that most of the authors and titles were French.

'Right then. What will you have? Vodka?'

She nodded. 'Fine. Don't get lost, will you?'

'No chance.' And she took his breath away by raising her face and taking his kiss straight on the mouth.

So she wanted it as much as he did. A pretty girl like that —you'd think they would be queuing up. But then she lived on her own with a kid. And worked in a flaming book-shop. Luke returned to his motorbike consoled by the conviction that, for once in Holtchester, he would shortly be doing the right thing. And enjoying it.

*

The immediate future held less promise for Hilde Tomlinson, seated now at the desk in her first floor office with her back to the darkening garden. The evening had begun well enough. She and Phyllis had arrived home at twenty past seven, earlier than she had dared to hope. Phyllis had scrutinized her under the hall lantern, her face tightening into Ward Sisterly concern.

'You look whacked.'

'I'll survive.' The drive from Heathrow always took the stuffing out of her.

'You should at least have a sherry, if you're hell-bent on going out again.'

'Defeat the object of the exercise. Can't concentrate if I'm tiddly. Come off it, Phyl. You know I like to get my papers into shape before my first full day back on the job. I'll make myself a cup of coffee at the clinic.'

With a quick squeeze of her friend's arm she had set off on the short walk to the clinic. Poor Phyllis. These brief, rushed holidays with a companion who was exhausted for the first couple of days and preoccupied by neglected duties for most of the remainder couldn't be much fun for her. When Hilde too had retired in a couple of years' time everything would be different. They could look forward to many shared months of foreign sunshine.

But for the present it was business as usual. Disraeli Gardens in near darkness was a far cry from Tuscany. The rain had lightened to a drizzle, but the sycamores dripped unpredictably and their leaves clogged the gutters. The parked cars were almost as shabby as the neglected terraces. Among the vehicles Hilde had noticed a vaguely familiar motorcycle. But she paid little attention to models or numberplates. Personal transport was to her a necessary but boring evil.

She had inspected the garden with more interest. The storms they had read about in Florence had battered the autumn crocuses and Michaelmas daisies. But the Japanese maples maintained a brave front against their background of conifer hedging, and fans of red-berried berberis enlivened the yellow brick walls. That hassle with the Authority over replanting was paying dividends. Who'd bully them when she was out of the system?

She had heard the typing as soon as she let herself into the building. So Luke Mason was availing himself of the facilities. Of course that motorcycle was familiar. He'd used Eileen Lethbridge's typewriter to type up his casenotes ever since she had complained about his appalling handwriting. Never caught him at it so late in the day before. But he'd probably accumulated a backlog in her absence and tomorrow was the day of judgement. Unless, of course, he was typing something quite unconnected with his clinic work. Well, let him get on with it. Through her contacts with the university where Luke had taken his degree, Hilde knew more of his academic and political activities than he supposed and tolerated them with less difficulty than he could have guessed. It was by no means unpleasant to be reminded of the socialist ideals of her own youth and the son who had adopted them. She'd look in later to remind Luke about locking up, but first she had more pressing business to attend to.

Without switching on the hall light, she had made her way to the small staff kitchen. As quietly as she could, she had prepared a mugful of black Nescafé and taken it upstairs to her office. A good two hours' work, she had guessed, scanning the contents of the bulky folder with an experienced eye. She'd feel a different woman when she'd got that lot into shape—pencilled action notes in margins, drafted replies to the most urgent letters and revised entries in her diary. But her first priority tonight, as after every period of leave, was to get in touch with Peter. And tonight she had dialled the familiar digits with more than usual anxiety.

'Out? Do you by any chance have a number?'

''Fraid not.' Cora Denny's detachment was overlaid with amusement. 'Said he'd dine in Town with some old school ch∶m or other after his session at St Tim's. Didn't pay much attention.'

When had she ever? It must be almost impossible to transmit significant messages through that thorny stockade. All the same, Peter should have made the effort to tell her about the closure. He'd be sick with worry till he got it over with. His work at Holtchester would suffer—must already be suffering. And the enemies of human resources therapy were gathered, ready to pounce at the first sign of clinical imcompetence.

She would ring him before breakfast the following morning. Fit in a half-hour meeting before their first clinic appointments. Warn him that if he didn't break the news to Cora that weekend she would seriously consider doing so herself. Meanwhile . . . but that precautionary measure would have to wait until Luke Mason was out of the building.

Martin Hobbs unwrapped his sandwiches in the empty cafeteria of Browne Community College. The other boys in the trampolining team had gone out to buy chips, but he didn't mind not being included. They were older and he had no friends among them. Not many friends altogether, if it came to that, apart from Susie. He punctured the carton of orange squash and drank thirstily. It had been a good practice. In his first term at Browne he'd thought diving was the most exciting sport in the world. Now he knew he was wrong. Trampolining was diving plus plus plus. Nothing could match the rapid succession of upward flights, the split-second battles against gravity as you tumbled and twisted high above your spotters. His eight-bounce routine was good, now he'd got his barani under control. Easily the best in his year. Good enough to be polished up for next

May's regional competition. Good enough as it stood for next week's sports gala.

'Is your mother coming to the gala?' Mr Henderson had been in the gym watching the practice, but he hadn't spoken to Martin until he bumped into him in the empty corridor outside the cafeteria. Hendy was careful like that. Knew the other kids had it in for teachers' pets.

'She didn't say. Usually works on Saturdays.'

Hendy made a funny face. 'Doesn't know what she'd be missing, I expect. I'll give her a ring myself this evening. Personal recommendation might do the trick.'

'Yes, sir . . . Oh, sir.' Courtesy titles were officially discouraged in the youth club, but Martin conformed to the peer group norm. 'You won't get Mum on the 'phone tonight. She'll be at the guidance clinic.'

The Acting Head's face wasn't funny any more. For a second he looked angry—angrier than Martin had ever seen him.

'At the Disraeli Gardens clinic? Are you sure? Didn't know they held evening sessions.'

'Don't, sir. She's using their typewriter.'

How daft it sounded when you said it out loud. Martin wanted very much to believe it, wanted to convince himself that the fibbing was over for good. It wasn't easy.

But Hendy was smiling again.

'Not to worry. I can ring her another time. Keep up the good work in the gym, won't you? No more problems at school?'

Martin shook his head, avoiding the kind hazel eyes. No problems that counted, since he'd stumbled upon his glorious secret. How long, he wondered, would he have to keep it to himself?

Left on his own again, Martin paused to count his money. Not bad for a Thursday. £3.25 in hand from this week's paper round and pocket money, plus £1 saved from last week. Enough to give his mother a surprise.

He went in search of it in the Art Room. As someone with a reputation for being good at painting, he had been dragooned into a group making sets for the forthcoming production of *The Mikado*. Messing about with poster colours on large surfaces wasn't his idea of fun. His skill and delight lay in meticulous sketches of small animals and birds. Mostly birds. He used to copy them from photographs in library books. But over the last couple of years he had been persuaded by his art teacher to sketch from life and imagination.

He'd spent a lot of time that spring and summer with a sketching group that met in Chess Wood, the nature reserve in which the school's Outdoor Pursuit Centre was located. That was where he'd got to know Susie Forbes, who belonged to another form in his unstreamed year group. They lived in the same estate and often cycled together to and from school. He'd have liked to join Susie in the jewellery group, which also met in the Art Room. But it was strictly a girls' preserve. They made pendants, rings and earrings. Mostly earrings. He was glad to see that Susie was working on her own this evening, filing and polishing, while two other girls were huddled over their enamel paints at a separate table.

'Like these?' Susie called out to him, pushing back her hair. It was dark, almost as dark as his mother's. But Susie's face was fuller, her chin less pointed.

Martin made a close inspection. The green and silver lizards lengthened Susie's neck. Made her look older than thirteen. Rather mysterious.

'Great. They suit you. Must have been a fiddly job.'

'You can say that again.'

But he was searching among the trays for something else. He couldn't find exactly what he wanted, so he settled for the closest approximation. A pair of tiny beech leaves cast in bronze.

'Still three-fifty?'

Susie nodded.

He counted out the money. His mother would almost certainly come to the gala if Hendy asked her specially. And he wanted more than anything for her to come wearing these earrings.

'For the new girlfriend?' Susie teased as she tore up some tissue paper.

'Just my mum,' Martin muttered. From the corner of his eye he could see Dave Wright sauntering towards them, a towel draped round his thick neck. Dave, whose house was almost opposite Martin's, was also an ex-pupil of Greenside Primary. During his lordship of its playground he had selected his neighbour for special harassment. Since his move to Browne a year ahead of the younger boy he had evidently found more amusing prey. Of recent weeks, however, he had begun to take an active interest in Susie.

'Haven't you bought your mother a pair like these before?' It had been before the summer holidays. Martin had hoped Susie wouldn't remember. They had suited his mother better than any of her other jewellery. The leaves—they were oak leaves that time—curled against her long neck like magical extensions of her hair. And she'd been so pleased with them, whirling him round and round in a dance in front of her wardrobe mirror. One of his most successful surprises.

'She lost them,' he mumbled quickly, but not quickly enough.

'Who lost what?' Dave Wright was at his elbow now, reeking of chloride and some fancy deodorant. Martin willed Susie not to answer, but it didn't work. People nearly always gave in to Dave. Girls especially.

'Martin's mum's lost a pair of earrings he bought her.'

'What—both of them? Now that *was* careless, wasn't it?' Dave reached over to pick up one of the little leaves. 'Bet they suited her an' all.'

'Shut up, will you.' Martin's voice squeaked treacherously.

The older boy let the trinket slide through his fingers and winked across the table at Susie. 'Sorry, I'm sure. All the same, Hobbs, I'd watch out for that ma of yours, if I were you. Doesn't exactly keep herself to herself from all I hear.'

'Lay off, Dave.' Susie made a business of wrapping up the purchase. 'Mrs Hobbs is all right. Bet you don't know the first thing about her private life.'

'Well, I'm a bit young for her, aren't I, love?' Dave moved round behind the table and caressed Susie's rump.

'Give over.' She elbowed him aside. Halfheartedly, thought Martin, his cheeks burning.

'My old woman's told me one or two interesting tales.' Dave opened a bag of crisps which he offered first to Susie, then to Martin. 'She used to work with Mrs H in the Foxwillow Arms. Reckon they'd some high times in that place. Maybe you and me's got more in common than we know about, mate.'

'Oh, go to Hell!' Martin stuffed the small parcel in his pocket, turned on his heel and hurried out of the room. It wasn't the first time he'd taken stick for his mother, but it had never been as bad as this. And never in front of Susie. His throat ached as he ran through the empty corridors. He tried hard to concentrate on the secret which would one day give Dave Wright and his sort their come-uppance. His mother didn't know he knew, and he'd meant to keep it that way. Let her think it came as a big surprise when she got round to telling him. But tonight he couldn't wait any longer. Not even till she came home. He'd go down to the clinic. Catch her as she was leaving. Make her tell him if he had to squeeze it out of her. Then they'd cycle home together. He'd give her the earrings and a tight, tight hug. It would be the happiest evening of his whole life.

The fantasy warmed him as he left the school buildings and ran across the damp tarmac to the cycle shed. As he fiddled with the padlock on his bike, the darkness, which used to terrify him, began to make him uneasy. It was the first evening he had left the youth club early and unaccompanied. As he rode out of the school gate his eyes scanned the row of parked cars for a balding head, a heavily jowled face. All clear. Only one was occupied, and that by a courting couple. The school loomed like a spaceship above its darkened grounds. He rode past, reassured by the light shining through the thin curtains of the Head's study. Nothing terrible could happen with John Henderson in control.

The rain held off as he rode downhill between the well-spaced villas of the modern parks and crescents, then along the level avenues of the closer-packed Victorian and Edwardian suburbs. He took a short cut that led to the service road behind the clinic. Looking up, he was dismayed by the light from Hilde Tomlinson's office window on the gable wall of the rear wing. So that's where his mother was. She had lied to him again. There had been worse lies, but this was bad enough. He had always hated to think of her going to the clinic. Telling Mrs Tomlinson all about their life together. Finding out what he had told Dr Denny about his bad dreams and makebelieve games. Oh, Dr Denny swore black and blue it wouldn't work that way. But Martin didn't trust him. You could see Mrs Tomlinson had him under her thumb. Besides, everything Martin said and did in treatment went down in casenotes that were kept in his file. Mrs T could read all about him. What was there to stop her passing it on to his mother?

'Doesn't tell me a thing about you, love,' she had assured him. 'Too busy trying to get me to spill my own beans.' He had laughed with her, but taken little comfort. She wasn't altogether to be trusted. Few grown-ups were.

He dismounted and walked slowly along the service road. The client's chair in the social worker's office was out of sight. But after several minutes' inspection he came to the conclusion that it was empty. The social worker's head was down, her writing arm active. Perhaps his mother had gone home already. He wheeled his bike into the alley at the side of the house and found hers. So she was somewhere in the building. Light was streaming into Dr Denny's office from the door connecting it with the waiting-room. He advanced a few paces. The Venetian blind behind the small side window of the waiting-room was not quite closed. Through the slats he could see Eileen Lethbridge's desk and her typewriter. Perhaps his mother had told him the truth, after all. Perhaps she was somewhere in the room.

He shivered. The effects of strenuous exercise were wearing off. The damp cold struck through his thin jerkin. He didn't fancy a long, lonely wait, but he didn't fancy going home to an empty house either. A ring on the doorbell would bring the wrath of old Ma Tomlinson down on his head. Perhaps there was some other way of getting inside. He retraced his steps down the side alley, which was walled off from the back garden, and turned right into the service road. He tried the gate in the high back fence and found it unbarred. Closing it quietly behind him, he ran as fast as he could up the path to the back of the house. The ground-floor windows were all closed and, he supposed, bolted. But the first-floor sash window of the staff lavatory had been left open. He considered. The sill looked accessible from the roof of the store-room below. There were no lights in the terrace behind him to suggest that it was overlooked from that direction, and it was out of sight from Mrs Tomlinson's office. His spirits rose. The prospect of combining a surprise appearance with a demonstration of developing athletic skills was irresistible.

And the plan worked. Within five minutes he was on the first-floor landing, with nothing to show for his mode of entry except a skinned thumb and a dirty mark on his right sleeve. He tiptoed downstairs, praying to be delivered from squeaky treads. Hilde Tomlinson coughed. He paused in the hall outside the closed door of the waiting-room. A strip of light showed underneath but there was no sound of typing.

He wondered if his mother would be angry. If she had someone in there with her. He opened the door of the psychiatrist's room. The hinge squeaked slightly. He waited. Nothing happened. He went inside. Looking round him at the couch, the low table, the sand tray, the dolls' house, he was suddenly overwhelmed by shame. His past indiscretions oppressed him. He'd grown out of this kids' stuff long ago. Told Dr Denny as much this summer. He'd been a fool to come back. It was all his mother's fault.

As he approached the door that led from the psychiatrist's office into the waiting-room he caught a whiff of her scent. And the old, babyish feelings rushed back with a vengeance. He wanted to butt his head against her, wailing out his anger and his desire. Then he heard her. Holding his breath, he inched round the edge of the door. She was standing with her back to him at one of the cabinets. She was reading something in one of the files. And she was laughing.

Luke Mason sighed with relief as he moved away from the last set of traffic-lights. Another minute and he'd be back at the clinic. Not before time. Must be all of half an hour since Cheryl put up her face for that sweet, unlooked-for kiss. He turned the corner into Disraeli Gardens a little too fast, narrowly missing the boy who ran into the road to wave him down. He braked hard, and leaped off his machine. The child might have been twelve or thirteen. He was about five feet tall and slim, with an open, freckled face.

'It's killed her!' he screamed. 'Don't you hear me? It's killed her!'

'What has?' Luke asked in the sure knowledge that he was precipitating the worst moment of his life.

'A tiger.' The boy was staring past him into the darkness. 'A bloody great tiger.'

CHAPTER 3

Luke hurried up the garden path, with Martin at his heels. The front door stood ajar. He turned the handle of the stained glass door behind it and came face to face with Hilde Tomlinson.

'Something horrible has happened,' she said. 'I've rung for the police.' Thrusting the boy among the blue-green grasses of her print wool bosom, Luke opened the door of the waiting-room. Cheryl lay slumped over the desk where he had left her working. An open file projected from under her curly black head. The typewriter, shrouded now, had been pushed to the back of the desk. Something shone among the pages that lay disordered on the carpet—a blood-stained breadknife that had spattered as it fell. He sickened at the sight of a remembered image. A red mark on a white sheet.

Detective Chief Inspector Baxter's hand bypassed the strategically positioned yoghurt and grasped the cream jug. He poured a generous dollop over his second helping of baked apple. As he ate he could see through the window behind his wife the dim outlines of their burdened orchard. Sarah, a handsome woman in her early forties, was wearing a coral two-piece that blended agreeably with her reddish-brown hair.

'Glad to be home, Dick?' she asked, draining her wineglass.

'What do you think?'

'I think these London conferences give you itchy feet.'

She had come nearer the truth than Richard Baxter cared to admit. Every time he met his ex-colleagues, the chorus of voices urging him to apply for transfer on promotion back to the Metropolitan Force seemed to grow in numbers and decibel ratings. He'd all the makings of a good Superintendent, they told him. The right track record. Steady head. Sense of humour. And the ability to distinguish wood from trees. A five-year stint in the provinces was long enough for a man of his calibre who was still well on the right side of fifty.

They had a case. Baxter knew his own metal. But he knew too that the move to the Mid-Anglian Constabulary and the consequent change-down to third gear had probably saved his life. And certainly saved his marriage.

'My turn to wash up,' he reminded Sarah, as he scraped his plate.

'Later. Let's enjoy our coffee.'

He followed her obediently to the comfortable old settee by the log fire, and let her pour him a large cupful. No need to watch the caffeine intake. No need for early sleep. Tomorrow they would lie in. It would be one of those rare weekdays when he and his wife, a part-time general practitioner, would both be off-duty.

'Fancy an evening in Cambridge tomorrow?' he asked, unfolding a copy of the *Evening News*. 'There's an Ayckbourn at the Arts Theatre.'

'And Mozart at King's. Toss for it?'

As Baxter dug for a coin, the telephone on the Sutherland table beside him began to ring.

'Yes . . . yes . . . yes.' Seeing his face harden, Sarah folded away the newspaper and reached for his free hand.

'What is it?'

'Murder.'

'And why do they have to have you?'

He replaced the receiver before replying. 'Because the Chief Constable says so. Reckons it's a tricky one. Crime was committed in Holtchester Child Guidance Clinic. Which could implicate the health, social and educational services—or so they tell me.'

'Thus undermining public confidence in public authority figures—the CC's favourite bugbear?'

'Exactly.' Baxter cupped his wife's creamy face in his palms and kissed her on the mouth. 'Don't wait up.'

She shook her head, kissing him back. 'Take care.'

Before leaving, he gulped down the remainder of his coffee. He might have to stay awake for rather a long time.

A three mile drive brought Baxter from the village of Kings Covert to the headquarters of the Mid-Anglian Constabulary in Holtchester. Two men awaited him. Detective Inspector William Armstrong's square face broke into a melon-slice grin. Disgustingly cheerful as usual, Baxter reflected, as he held open the front passenger door of his silver Rover. Thank God, Bill knew him well enough to inhibit his habitual chatter on the short trip to Disraeli Gardens. And Detective-Sergeant Colin Short, relegated to the back seat, took his cue from his superiors and surveyed without comment the succession of almost empty streets.

On arrival, Baxter paused briefly to contemplate the 1850-ish frontage of the child guidance clinic. A nice house in its day, but deteriorating fast and probably doomed to demolition by the end of the century. Local conservationists had their work cut out staving off redevelopment of the seventeenth-century town centre.

Dr Green, the police surgeon, met them in the hall.

'It's hospital for this lad,' he muttered, jerking his head towards a blanketed figure watched over by a woman constable. 'Clinical shock. Poor kid found his mother, they tell me. Ambulance is on its way. You'll have to get his statement tomorrow.'

Baxter nodded. Over the five years of their working relationship he had learnt to respect Green's judgement. He followed the doctor into the waiting-room, where the Scene of Crimes team was already at work. A photographer blocked their view of the dead woman.

'Name of Cheryl Hobbs, isn't it?' he asked the uniformed sergeant. 'What's she doing here?'

'Spot of typing, it would seem. Her kid used to have treatment here, I believe.'

'Finished with her now, sir,' the photographer called out. Dr Green stepped forward and lifted Cheryl's head.

Baxter looked into a wide-eyed pointed face, the face of a sacrificial offering.

'Strangulation?' he asked, returning the stare of the grey eyes.

'Looks like it. Hardly any bleeding from the stab wounds.'

Baxter's eye caught the glint of the knife. So someone had wanted to make assurance double sure. Or got a kick out of those repeated lunges at chest and throat. But a breadknife wasn't the usual weapon for a ritual killing. And the girl's jeans were fully zippered and buttoned. No obvious sign of sexual interference.

He crossed the room and entered the Medical Director's office.

'Convenient getaway.' He drew Armstrong's attention to the side door leading to the alley.

'Funny arrangement, that.'

'You see all sorts of gimcrack conversions in these Victorian properties. Dare say the two rooms were let as a flatlet when the place was in private hands. Anyhow, we'd better clear out and leave the lads to their fingerprinting and snapshots.'

A constable stood guard over the playroom where Hilde Tomlinson and Luke Mason awaited interrogation. The senior social worker and her trainee sat several yards apart. Luke was making a show of reading his paperback but Hilde sat upright, contemplating the half-expunged crayon scribbles on the wall opposite. Introductions over, Baxter turned to her.

'Can we find somewhere more comfortable to talk?'

'The Medical Director's room?'

'Out of bounds for the time being, I'm afraid.'

'Really?' Hilde's fingers tightened on the handle of her handbag. 'My office then? It's on the first floor.'

She remained tense in her personal domain, sitting well forward on one of the easy chairs normally reserved for clients and fidgeting with the car coat that she wore slung over her shoulders. Baxter took her chair behind the well-ordered desk and Armstrong a second hard chair which he positioned at right angles to his superior's. Detective-Sergeant Short hovered expectantly.

'Routine questions first, if you don't mind,' Baxter began. 'May I have the home address and telephone number of the Medical Director?'

'Dr Denny's not at home this evening. And I've already left a message . . .'

'But messages don't always get through as quickly as one could wish. I'd rather like to send a car round. So if you please . . .'

She relayed the information, colouring a little. Fully aware, no doubt, that his object was to forestall collusion. 'And could you let me know the name of Mrs Hobbs's adult next-of-kin?'

'There's one unmarried sister. A Miss Taylor. Lives in Mere Street, I believe. And there's the ex-husband, of course. He's a bus driver. Don't know if you'd want to contact him. But if you do, Angliabus should be able to help.'

Baxter scribbled brief notes of instruction and passed them to Colin Short, who hurried from the room.

'Very many thanks. Now we'd better get back to business. May I have your full name?'

'Hilde Renate Tomlinson.'

'*Renate*. Are you German by birth?'

She shook her neat grey head. 'Austrian.' Her consonants

were unusually precise, but otherwise the accent could be
that of any well-educated woman from the Home Counties.
'We came to London in 'thirty-nine when I was eleven.' Her
brown eyes flickered briefly above her half-lenses as he did
the sum. Couldn't have been an easy year for an immigrant
child with a German accent. But the cleanly sculpted face
and the thick body beneath the vivid dress had the strength
of a survivor.

Hilde gave her evidence lucidly and, for the most part,
without overt emotion. Armstrong was the first to draw
blood.

'You believed Mr Mason to be in the waiting-room when
you arrived in the clinic at 7.25, but you weren't concerned
about what he might be up to?'

'I had no reason to be.'

'But on your own admission Mr Mason wasn't an ideal
trainee. And you'd left him unsupervised for a whole week.'
Armstrong's Ulster Presbyterian conscience was genuinely
stirred.

'That's not true. Luke had been assigned a light case-load.
And he'd been instructed to seek advice on any difficulty
from Dr Denny or from Mrs Groundstock, one of the district
social workers, who was covering emergencies.'

'How could you be sure he would ask for advice?'

'I couldn't.' She was flushed now. 'But Luke wasn't
foolhardy and he badly wanted a pass mark. Still does, I
dare say. Beyond that, it was a matter of trust.' Her voice
cracked on the word.

'Misplaced trust, it would seem?'

'Don't rub it in, Inspector.' Baxter noticed for the first
time how tired she looked under the light tan. There were
patches of white round her eyes and mouth. And tears in
her eyes. For herself or Cheryl Hobbs or someone else again?
He reclaimed the questioning.

The senior social worker's account of her evening's work
was marked by a scrupulous concern for client confiden-

tiality which Baxter noted with interest, but did not challenge. The sight of the open drawer in the filing-cabinet and the open file under Cheryl's body might well have pained her more than the sight of the dead woman. Assuming she was telling the truth about the discovery. The sight of the open window in the staff lavatory which she visited at a time she could not specify had, however, failed to disturb her. People were careless about such things.

'What finally brought you downstairs?'

'A scream. And almost immediately the slam of a door.'

'Did you notice the time?'

'Eight-nineteen.'

'Precisely?'

She shrugged, paler now. 'It struck me that it might be important to note the time. I've a reliable watch.'

'And then?'

'Then I switched on the landing light and ran downstairs as fast as I could.'

'Taking your handbag?'

'Yes.' The question surprised, but didn't embarrass her. 'Force of habit. Take it everywhere I go when I'm away from home. My mother used to lecture me on the evil of exposing others to temptation.'

'May I see?' Baxter asked, walking across to her. She hesitated briefly, then handed the bag over. It was tan in colour, made out of some expensive, soft leather and silk lined. He made a quick visual inspection of the kid gloves, Italian and British currency, credit cards, passport and photograph of a young, dark-haired family, thanked her, and returned to his seat.

'You ran downstairs. What next?'

'I switched on the light in the hall, opened the waiting-room door and found the body, slumped over the desk.'

'You recognized Mrs Hobbs?'

'Yes.'

'But you didn't touch her?'

She shook her head. 'I went straight through to Dr Denny's room and rang the police and Dr Denny's house. In that order. I closed the door from the waiting-room to the hall.'

'Why?'

'In case someone slipped past me. Someone who couldn't take it . . . I didn't realize the boy had already seen her. And I opened the front door so that the police could get in without difficulty. The doorbell was erratic. Then I sat down on the bottom step of the stairs and waited. I checked my watch again. It was eight twenty-four.'

'How long before Luke came back with the boy?'

'Another five minutes. Eight twenty-nine. And the uniformed policemen were here almost immediately after that.'

Could do better, Baxter reflected, composing a sharp memo to the Superintendent.

'You knew Cheryl Hobbs for some time?' he asked, changing course with a rapidity that created havoc with Armstrong's shorthand paragraphing.

'Three years.'

'You knew her pretty well, then.'

Hilde grimaced. 'Yes and no.'

'Can you expand on that?'

'I didn't know her well in any meaningful sense. She wouldn't let me come close enough.'

'Why was that?'

She laughed. 'Oh, she was quite honest about it. She distrusted women, especially older women. She'd had a bad relationship with her own mother.'

'I see. Did you *like* Cheryl Hobbs, Mrs Tomlinson?'

Hilde flushed again. 'Not exactly. She made it difficult at times. But I felt some affinity for her.'

'Really?'

'She reminded me of myself as an adolescent. I was a prickly little thing in those days.'

'Could you have killed her?'

Her brown eyes met Baxter's.

'In extreme circumstances, yes. So, I dare say, could you, Chief Inspector. But such circumstances didn't obtain.'

'Can you think of anyone who might have had a grudge against her?'

'No.' She considered. 'There had been lovers, of course. She'd been quite promiscuous in her teens and even during her marriage. Made no bones about it. Surprising, really, that she stayed married for four years. After the divorce she had settled down. Or so she wanted me to believe. There was a current boyfriend in London. Well-heeled, I gathered. And I feel sure there were others. But she named no names and I didn't press her. She was very cagey.'

'Why, do you think?'

'She was worried sick about losing custody of her son. Especially now that her husband had remarried and moved back into the area.'

'Would you say she loved the boy?'

'After her fashion.' Hilde played with the rings on her strong hands. 'The fashion of a spoilt child. She was inconsistent. But she certainly wouldn't have given him up without a struggle.'

Baxter thanked her. Armstrong reread the statement which she agreed to sign on the following day and escorted her downstairs. In his absence, the Chief Inspector strolled across to the window. The rain had stopped now, and the moon was rising above the roofscape into a many-toned inky sky. He turned to survey the room. Apart from the desk and chairs the only item of furniture was a small bookcase. His eye scanned the titles and lit on *Human Resources Therapy: A Symposium* edited by Peter Denny and Hilde Renate Tomlinson. He flicked through the 700-odd pages which were littered with the abbreviations so typical of scientific texts. Among these preponderated the initials HRT, obviously standing for Human Resources Therapy, but also—he

realized with a jolt—matching Hilde Renate Tomlinson.
So the social worker had given her name to a baby that
linked her with at least one of her professional colleagues.
A baby she probably wouldn't give up without some sort of
struggle.

Luke Mason, thin and sallow-complexioned, leant back in
the easy chair Hilde had vacated and crossed his legs with
a show of nonchalance. Baxter noted that he made no move
to unbutton his duffel coat.

'Mind if I smoke?' The detective handed over an ashtray
and caught the whiff of alcohol. The young man's tired face
reinforced his own weariness and his consciousness of hard
tasks ahead. He set a brisk pace in interrogation, and Mason
barked out a bald but reasonably coherent account of his
day's activities.

'So you went out about 7.55 to buy the vodka. Why The
Blue Waggon? There are other pubs nearer the clinic.'

He shrugged. 'Force of habit. Went there most days.'

'How long did it take to make the purchase?'

'Five minutes, maybe. There was quite a queue.'

'And you had a drink when you were there?'

'Yeah. Small vodka.'

'Why?'

'Why the hell do you think? I wanted one. Besides, I
didn't want to go back too soon. Cheryl had a fair bit of
typing and correction left to do.'

'See anyone you knew in the pub? You realize we'll have
to check up.'

Mason laughed. 'Feel free. Matter of fact, I complained
to the landlord.'

'About your drink?'

'About the contraceptive machine in the gents. It didn't
deliver. One of life's little ironies, don't you think?'

Baxter ignored the note of self-pity and Armstrong's
throat-clearings.

'How long altogether were you in the pub?'

'Oh I don't know. Ten or twelve minutes, I dare say.'

'And then?'

'Then I went back to my digs. Thought there were some condoms in my chest-of-drawers.'

'And were there?'

'Uh-huh.'

'See anyone when you were there?'

'No such luck. It was soap opera time on the box and the old couple who own the house had it on full blast. They're both pretty hard of hearing.'

'Happen to recall any of the dialogue?' Mason shook his head. 'That crap goes in one ear and out the other.'

Armstrong accepted his senior's unspoken invitation to take over the questioning. 'Then you came back here?'

Mason shook his head. 'Meant to, but the bike wouldn't start. Kicked like crazy, but it's only a two-stroke and I flooded the crankcase. So I had to sort that out.'

'How long did all that take?'

'Ten minutes or more.'

'Frustrating. But eventually you rode back, intending to have sexual intercourse with Mrs Hobbs?'

'Hoping, you bloody swine, just hoping. Can't you understand that?'

'We'll do our best to understand,' Baxter cut in quickly. 'But it would help if you toned down your language.'

'Sorry.' It was a shoddy synonym for despair.

'Had Mrs Hobbs given you reason to believe she wanted you to make love to her?' Baxter asked gently.

'I thought so.' A long silence.

'Go on.'

'Do I have to?'

'If you please.'

Luke's hands clamped the review copy of *Personal Services and Public Humiliation* as he itemized those scattered words and actions of Cheryl's that had seemed to signal her desire.

Then his rage re-ignited. 'I suppose you want me to say I'm responsible.'

'For what?'

'For her d . . .' He couldn't get his tongue round the word. 'For-landing her in this . . . bloody awful mess.'

He began to sob.

'Vodka on an empty stomach,' Armstrong muttered.

'Well, *are* you responsible?' Baxter persisted.

'Of course not. I didn't know she was going to fish out that bloody file, did I? But she'd a perfect right. And anyone who killed her for it was a patho. Well, wasn't he?' Mason stuffed the paperback into his briefcase, snapped it shut, and glared at the Chief Inspector. An angry and guilty child, demanding reassurance.

'Perhaps he was a patho, perhaps not. For all we know, Mrs Hobbs may have been killed for a reason that had nothing to do with her file. Or with the clinic.'

Relief lit up the young man's sallow face. 'Funny, I never thought of that.'

'Understandable,' Armstrong reassured him. 'Not your job, is it? You're not trained up to it.'

'No, thank God.'

'Tell us what happened when you got back to Disraeli Gardens,' Baxter prompted.

'I came round the corner in a hurry. Realized it was getting on for 8.30. Martin Hobbs was in the roadway and I nearly ran him down.'

'You knew him?'

'Not till he opened his mouth. Then I realized . . .'

'What did he say? Can you remember the exact words?'

As if Luke could think clearly of anything else.

'He said: "It's killed her. Don't you hear me? It's killed her." "What has?" I asked him. "A tiger," he said. "A bloody great tiger."'

'What did you make of that?'

'Hardly the moment for textual analysis, Chief Inspector.

Or so it seemed at the time. I hustled the kid back into the clinic as fast as I could.' A wry smile. 'To find that Hilde Tomlinson had got everything under control.'

'What do you mean by that?'

'Nothing, really. Hilde's one of those born managers. Keeps her cool in crises. She said something horrible had happened, but she'd phoned the police.'

'*Only* the police?'

Luke nodded. 'Then she took charge of the boy and I went in to look at Cheryl.' He covered his mouth.

'You didn't touch anything?'

He shook his head. 'Couldn't bear to. When I saw the breadknife on the floor I felt sure she was dead. Then Hilde called me out and asked me to put my duffel round the kid's legs. He was shaking. She'd already got her own coat and gloves on to him. The three of us waited till the police came.'

'You'd time to think about the tiger story then. Perhaps you talked about it to Mrs Tomlinson?'

'No. I told Hilde briefly why I'd invited Cheryl to the clinic and why I'd left her. Hilde said she'd been working in her room till a noise had disturbed her. We agreed to leave it at that until the police came. For the kid's sake.'

'For your sake, too?'

'Perhaps. I was in no mood for a cross-examination.'

'Did Mrs Tomlinson seem angry?'

'She didn't, come to think of it. Not as much as one might have expected, anyhow. A bit tense and preoccupied, I'd say.'

'The tiger story—you've had time to think it over. What do you make of it now?'

Luke shrugged. 'Fantasy—what else? Kid had a history of emotional disturbance. Bad dreams, too, I seem to remember. Reckon he'd seen or done something too scary to come to terms with. So he flipped into a jungle nightmare.'

'Retrieved from the depths of the Freudian unconscious?' Baxter needled.

'From the depths of TV or video nasties, more like,' Mason snapped. 'Lonely kids lap up more than their fair share.'

'I dare say.' Baxter realized that the young man before him would derive considerable comfort from a verdict against the System. He had found it hard to abandon his own chequerboard image of the human game in favour of the grey mists of multiple motivation.

'Have you finished with me?' Luke asked, when he had listened to Armstrong's report of his evidence.

'For the present.' Baxter stood up. 'You can sign your statement at the police station tomorrow morning. But I'd be glad if you stayed on in Holtchester for the time being.'

'Very well.' Luke swayed a little as he followed Armstrong downstairs. The prospect of an extended stay was bleak enough. But as he watched the loaded stretcher being lifted into the police van, he could envisage no more comforting alternative.

CHAPTER 4

By ten-thirty Baxter, sitting at the desk in his own office, was beginning to feel in command of the investigation. He'd set up an incident room and released a media statement which omitted the name of the victim.

'Something for you to chew on.' He pushed a computer print-out across the desk to Armstrong. 'The Mason story.'

'Uh-huh.' Bill spoke through a mouthful of crisps. 'Student demagogue right from his fresher days, I see . . . Organizing sit-ins, lock-outs . . . Generally wasting the tax-payer's money, cheeky bastard.'

'Clever bastard too, don't you think? He's kept on the

right side of the law this last couple of years. And he seems to be taking the community social work thing seriously. Besides, he knows what we have against him. Could just have cooked us up the alibi that matches the image.'

'Could have. But my money's on young Hobbs. Boy's sick, if you ask me. Tiger story's crazy, telly or no telly. And shrinks don't see you for months on end unless something's badly wrong, I reckon. Not in the NHS anyway. Think the kid might have done it? Physically, I mean.'

'Let's see.' Baxter dialled the pathologist, and repeated his preliminary findings as much for his own benefit as Armstrong's. 'Killed where she sat, you think? Manual strangulation from behind. Right-handed assailant possibly wearing· gloves. Smudged fingerprints on the knife to be matched with the neck marks. Semen stains, but they've still to be time-tested.'

'If we get the kid fingerprinted tomorrow we might sew the whole thing up,' Armstrong observed hopefully. He had promised to take his eldest to Holtchester United's home game that Saturday.

'Or again we might not,' his senior observed with the smug look that Armstrong's Derry grandmother used to bestow on him. It was the visual equivalent of her favourite proverb: 'The old dog for the hard road and the pup for the path.' Sick-making at fifteen—more so at thirty-five.

It was ten past eleven when Peter Denny was shown into the office. The psychiatrist's face was expressionless as he took a seat. His expensive tweed suit hung loosely, hinting at recent weight loss.

'Good of you to come,' Baxter murmured.

'Appalling business.' Denny ran a helpless hand through his thinning hair. 'Haven't really taken it in.'

'Not surprised. But you'll be as keen as I am to deal with matters expeditiously at the end of a busy day. You won't mind if we plunge in at the deep end?'

'Please do.' Denny leant forward in the pose of the professional listener.

'When did you last see Mrs Hobbs?'

'Not sure I can help you much there. Didn't see her regularly, you know. We operate as a team. One person to treat the child: someone else—maybe two people—to do casework with the parent or parents. No split loyalties. The arrangement's meant to inspire confidence. *Confidence!*' A harsh bark. 'Sorry, gentlemen.'

'Please go on.'

'Every so often in the treatment of a case we have review meetings. Child, parent or parents and guidance team workers all attend. We held a review of the Tomlinson case last summer. Mid-June, I think. Mrs Hobbs and Martin were there, along with Hilde Tomlinson and myself. That would be the last time I saw the poor girl.'

'Had that meeting any specific purpose?'

'Yes—to decide whether we should stop Martin's treatment.'

'Was he cured?'

The psychiatrist laughed. 'Would it were so simple. The outcome of psychotherapy's never clearcut, whatever the behaviourists may tell you. Martin's initial symptoms didn't evaporate. But by last summer they were definitely alleviated.'

'Can you be more explicit, Dr Denny?'

'Not without breaching professional ethics. Mrs Hobbs may be dead, but her son isn't. As a doctor, I've a duty to withhold information which in non-medical hands might be used to damage the reputation, even the mental health, of and ex-patient.'

'Very well,' Baxter spoke very quietly. 'But haven't you also a duty to consider the boy's physical safety.'

'I don't . . .'

'Isn't it obvious? The boy may have seen the murderer. And been seen. The clinic file relating to the case was found under the victim's body. When the forensic tests are complete, I shall certainly wish to read it. With your permission. You are probably aware that the British Medical Association has an agreement with the Chief Constables to make medical records available to senior police officers investigating serious crimes.'

'What can I say?' Denny spread out long, elegant fingers. 'I can only ask you to exercise discretion—and charity. We try to enter into the states of mind of our patients as they are disclosed. So we make little attempt in our therapeutic records to distinguish fact from fantasy. As you must.'

Baxter grunted. 'I'll take that hurdle when it comes. About this June meeting . . .'

'Yes, well. When Martin was first referred his presenting symptoms were troubling dreams, fear of the dark and acute anxiety about school attendance. By last June, all three problems had seemingly been reduced to normal proportions.'

'Seemingly?'

'Hilde and I suspected prevarication. Collusion between the boy and his mother to paint a rosy picture. Mrs Hobbs had never been forthcoming and over the previous two or three months Martin had been noticeably more guarded in his sessions with me.'

'So you were against the termination of treatment?'

'I'd have liked the boy to attend for a few more months. I anticipated problems at the beginning of the following school year—always a bad time for school refusers.'

'But you were persuaded to let him go?'

'Any other decision would have been counterproductive. Mrs H was openly hostile about treatment and Martin was ambivalent. Under pressure, I thought.'

'From mother?'

'And the school. Teachers playing at therapy tend to get over-involved, and John Henderson's no exception. He made it pretty clear to Jane Gordon—and to the boy, I suspect—that he regarded the clinic's continued involvement as superfluous.'

'Did this surprise you?'

'A little. Henderson's built up a good pastoral care service at Browne, and they don't refer cases to us unless they have to. But we've had reasonable cooperation from them in the past over kids already in treatment.'

'Did you know Mrs Hobbs would be coming to the clinic this evening?'

'Good God, no. I'm still in the dark about that. Who set it up?'

'Mr Mason. Seems he invited her to use the secretary's typewriter. But can we get back to the events of your day?'

'I don't . . .' Peter Denny twisted his wedding ring. 'Oh well, I suppose you have a right . . .'

'We should be grateful.'

'I treated four children this morning. Had a sandwich lunch in my office and left the clinic about one-thirty. The secretary will be able to confirm that.'

'And then?'

Denny blew his nose. 'I've lost a job . . . am in process of losing a job . . . in London. They're closing the child psychiatry unit at St Timothy's. Winding down gradually. I worked four half-day sessions for them—two on Mondays, plus Thursday and Friday afternoons. The Thursday sessions were axed six weeks ago, Friday afternoons finished last week and the Monday sessions stop at Christmas.'

'So you've unexpected time on your hands?'

Baxter's sympathy was tinged with envy of those professionals who could make an adequate living out of part-time employment.

'Yes. I didn't quite know what to do with it. You'll wonder why I didn't spend my Thursday afternoons at home?'

'Will I?' Funny sort of response. But shrinks were in the business of reading people's minds.

'Truth of the matter is I hadn't broken the news to my wife.'

'I see.' The psychiatrist might have opened the gate to a highly rewarding garden path, but it was not one Baxter intended to explore that evening.

'Where *did* you go this afternoon?'

'To London as usual. I've a book nearing completion. One of three joint efforts with Hilde Tomlinson. I've been spending these last six weeks on it. Revising and checking up references in various libraries.'

'Which one did you visit today?'

'The Senate House Library—part of London University. It's in Malet Street. Bloomsbury.'

'You drove straight there?'

'As far as Euston. Parked in the big multi-storey near the station. Walked the rest of the way.'

'What do you drive?'

'A red Maestro. Bought it when they first came out. Took quite a lot of ribbing from my colleagues over it. Unconscious urge to dominate and all that.'

'So you worked in the Senate House Library this afternoon.' Baxter was in no mood for diversion. 'Talk to anyone?'

'It's not encouraged. Besides, I didn't see anyone I knew. Job took longer than I'd expected, but I wasn't sorry. Fellow I usually dined with in Soho wasn't available. Name of Pyke —you'll want his number, I suppose? It was around seven when I finished at the library. Wasn't hungry, but I'd worked up a thirst. Stopped at a pub in Tottenham Court Road for a lager.'

'Which one?'

'Damned if I can remember the name. Know it was near Goodge Street station—I took the tube back to the car park. But what the hell—a traditional name, something monarchical.'

'The George?'

'No, not quite. But something equally commonplace. The Edward—the King Edward. I couldn't help thinking of the potato.'

'Were they busy?'

'Place was seething. Mostly tourists, I gathered, from the b-and-b hotels in the vicinity. No familiar faces—it's not one of my regular haunts.'

'Stay long?'

'Can't have. It was a quarter to eight when I clocked out of the car park.'

'Kept the ticket?'

'No such luck. I'm untidy in most ways but I don't keep things like that. My mother used to grind on about cluttering oneself up with unnecessary rubbish.'

'Go on, please.'

'I drove out of Town and along the A.10. Traffic was light by then so I made good speed. Too good. You must think I'm a bloody coward . . .'

'Does it matter if I do?'

Denny laughed. 'Suppose not. Anyhow, I realized I must break the news to my wife over the weekend, but I couldn't face the prospect this evening. It would be easier tomorrow when Hilde Tomlinson was back from leave and available to hold my hand. Hilde's very good at handholding— metaphorically speaking.'

'We have met.' Baxter wished he could make a photographic record of Armstrong's astonishment.

'Apologies, Chief Inspector. You must be bored stiff.'

'Only weary. You didn't know Mrs Tomlinson would be visiting the clinic this evening?'

'Suspected she might. But I knew she'd be whacked. Didn't want to take advantage . . .'

'I see. You drove up the A.10?'

'Almost as far as Royston. Then I took the B road for Hunters Rise. Thought I'd eat at the Ruffled Feathers—I expect you've been there.'

'Once or twice. It's got quite a reputation, hasn't it? But art deco and chrome are too flash for my taste.'

'And mine. The brasserie's like that, but the main restaurant's quite trad. And the grills are good value. I use it every so often when I'm on my tod. None of Cora's crowd go there. And before you ask me I didn't see a soul I knew this evening. I had a pernod and ordered my steak in the brasserie. But it was hellishly noisy and crowded with Sloane Rangers. So I asked them to bring my food into the restaurant, which was almost empty.'

'When did you leave?'

'Ten-twenty—something like that. Wanted to get home at my usual Thursday time.'

The recap was quick and relatively painless.

'Good. Now, I don't want to detain you unnecessarily, but we'll have to make a thorough search of the clinic premises. I'd like to clarify procedure . . .'

'Very well. Anything to clear the business up as fast as possible . . .'

'I've given instructions that files and other confidential papers should be left untouched. Apart from the Hobbs file, which has already been removed. I'll need the help of you and your colleagues tomorrow in sifting sensitive from non-sensitive papers. And I'd like all clinic staff to hold themselves available for interview throughout the day.'

'So we'll have to cancel appointments?'

'Just for Friday.'

'If we must, we must, I suppose. Poor Hilde will be terribly upset about this mess. Hardly a good advertisement for human resources therapy.'

Some day soon, Baxter thought as the psychiatrist left his office, I'll find out what those three bloody words mean. Read a Denny and Tomlinson textbook from cover to cover if necessary. But not tonight.

Before leaving the station, he rang Holtchester District Hospital and heard what he wanted to hear. Martin Hobbs was asleep under sedation. An interview would be neither desirable nor profitable before morning. But hospital mornings come early and there was another visit to be fitted in first. Baxter arranged a six o'clock rendezvous with Armstrong before heading for his home in Kings Covert and Sarah's drowsy embrace.

Let not your heart be troubled. Freda Taylor had not yet torn yesterday's scriptural quotation off the calendar on her mantelpiece. To judge by her placid reception of the two detectives who presented themselves on her doorstep at 6.10 am, she had made the text her own. She ushered her callers into a cluttered living-room and switched on one bar of the electric fire. A knitting-machine stood on the dining-table below the window and the shelves in the alcoves on either side of the fireplace were stacked high with woollen garments wrapped in polythene.

'Something's happened to Cheryl, hasn't it?' Freda asked as they sat down. The face above her buttoned-up maroon housecoat was long and large-featured. But the high cheekbones and slanted eyes gave credence to her kinship with the woman she would be asked to identify.

'Why should you say that?'

'No real reason. Just this feeling that she's been heading for trouble. Taking too many risks.'

'What kind of risks?'

Freda shook her head. 'I don't know. If I had, I might have been able to help. But Cheryl wouldn't stand for meddling. And I wanted to maintain some sort of contact— for the boy's sake as much as hers. Tell me what's happened.'

Baxter paraphrased the contents of the press release. The woman opposite covered her face for a few seconds, exposing a bandage on her left wrist. But when she removed her hands her eyes were dry.

'Poor Cheryl. I used to pray for her,' she said in the flat voice of someone habituated to failure.

'You still could,' Armstrong suggested.

Freda shook her head. 'She's in the Lord's hands now. Where's Martin?'

Baxter explained, adding that he would like her to be present at his interview with the boy. The identification of the body must wait.

'The hospital won't be ready for us until after seven. In the meantime, I'd be grateful if you would answer a few questions.'

'May I make myself decent?'

'Of course.'

'Look.' Armstrong indicated a packaged sweater in the same pattern as the dead woman's.

The beige knitted suit that Freda Taylor wore on her return was unadorned and unbecoming to her olive complexion. She was clutching a tissue.

'Sorry. I'm just beginning to take it in.' She mopped her eyes.

'Cup of tea?' Armstrong suggested. She led the way into a narrow slip of a kitchen. He followed on her heels.

'Will you join me?'

'I wouldn't say no. Whoops!' He made a grab for the electric kettle before it crashed to the floor.

'Thanks.' His hostess shook a bandaged wrist. 'This sprain's nearly better, but every so often it lets me down.'

'You're left-handed, I see.'

'To my mother's shame. She spent hours trying to change me over. Got my first infant school teacher on to her side. Without success. Thank goodness people are more tolerant these days. Poor Martin's had enough to put up with without that sort of pressure.'

'Boy's left-handed too, is he?' Armstrong watched with approval as she heated the pot.

'Mm-hm. I tell him it's the artistic temperament.' She managed the ghost of a smile.

Baxter heard the words with considerable relief. He accepted a cup of tea and a Marie biscuit. The tensions of the chase were apt to set his stomach acids flowing.

'Now for some questions, if you please.' He spoke briskly. 'When did you last see your sister?'

'About midnight last Sunday.'

'You're quite sure?'

'Positive. Cheryl went up to London three or four times a month. On a Thursday or a Sunday. If it was on Sunday Martin usually spent the day with me. She'd call for him on her way home. There's a shortcut from the station to this part of town. She'd usually ten minutes to spare here before they left for the last bus home.'

'Any idea what she did in London?'

Freda shook her head. '"Business and pleasure" was the only answer I ever got. Tight as a clam, was Cheryl, when she wanted to be. I know she picked up the odd book for the Poulencs. But there was more to it than that. "Tell you when I'm married," she'd say.'

'Planning to remarry, was she?' Baxter's antennae quivered. 'When did she first tell you about that?'

'About four or five weeks ago. Early September. Steve Hobbs had just come back from his holiday. Brown as a berry, he was, when he came·round here the following Monday.'

'Steve Hobbs. Cheryl's ex-husband. He visited you regularly?'

'Almost every week this last couple of years. Oh, there wasn't anything between us, if that's what you're thinking. I don't hold with divorce but Steve's second wife's a good woman. Used to go to our chapel. Steve came to ask after Martin. Eager for any scrap of news. He may have his faults, but he's crazy about that boy.'

'Did you tell him straight away about your sister's marriage plans?'

'Yes. I thought it was best to warn him. Anyhow, Cheryl wanted him to know. Reckoned it would put paid to any ideas he might have of getting custody of Martin. Poor Steve.'

'Did you ever invite Mr Hobbs over here on a Thursday or Sunday to be with his son?'

'I thought about it. Steve had a legal right to access, after all. But whenever I put the idea to Martin, he panicked. Got sick with fear. Quite literally. Always had this trouble with his nerves, you see, long before they sent him to the clinic. So after two or three attempts I gave up. Reckoned that as Martin grew up his curiosity would get the better of him. That he'd want to see if his Dad was as bad as Cheryl had made out to him. Then something happened to make me change my mind.'

'Uh-huh?' It was clear that Freda was in need of the second cup of tea she poured herself after the men had refused.

'It was nine or ten weeks ago. Towards the end of the boy's summer term. He was helping me wash up the supper dishes. Telling me all about a medal he'd won for swimming.'

'"Your Dad'll be pleased to hear that," I said.

'Martin turned on me double quick. Grabbed my wrist like a vice—just as well it wasn't sprained then. "For God's sake, Auntie," he said, "don't talk about that man as if he was my father. I know for a fact he's not."

'"Whoever gave you that idea?" I asked. "Not your mother, surely?"

'The boy shook his head then. Seemed embarrassed. "Shouldn't have said anything yet," he said. "Not until it's out in the open. Don't mention it to Mum, will you?"

'"Certainly not," I said. "Particularly as there isn't a word of truth in the story. And the sooner you get it out of your head, the better."'

'How could you be sure?' Armstrong asked.

'Steve's changed a lot since he's put on weight, but in his

younger days he was the image of Martin. There was no arguing with the boy when he'd got this bee in his bonnet, but I fished out some old photographs and left them lying about the house in time for his next visit.'

'Do any good?'

'I thought so at first when they disappeared. Then I found them torn up into tiny pieces in the dustbin. That really upset me at the time. Seemed almost like murder.' Freda's long face crumpled, but she rallied quickly.

The story of her earlier relationship with Cheryl was far from unusual. The plain firstborn daughter had disappointed both parents. The pretty little sister, eight years younger, had enchanted her extrovert father and driven a wedge into an already rickety marriage. Less usual were the circumstances of the father's death from heart failure in the middle of a romp with sixteen-year-old Cheryl. And the intensity of the mother's unforgiving anger.

Cheryl had left school soon afterwards. She had found work, first as a chambermaid, later as a receptionist, at the Foxwillow Arms, a local hotel. At 20 she had married a local car trader and motor mechanic, by whom she was already pregnant. Five years later Steve's small business went on the rocks and with it the marriage. Failure, Freda hinted, was an unforgivable sin in Cheryl's book. After the divorce she had temporarily disappeared from her sister's life.

'I felt terrible, not knowing how she was managing.' Freda twisted the bracelet of her wristwatch. 'But it was Mum. Wouldn't have anything to do with Cheryl once she heard about the divorce. We'd moved here, Mum and I, after Dad died. He'd owned a hardware business, but it was going downhill and we had to sell. We bought this little place with our share of the proceeds. Mum was poorly, even then. Couldn't be left on her own. I wasn't trained for anything except the business, but luckily I was always good at knitting.'

'When did you renew contact with your sister?' Baxter asked.

'About six years ago when Martin was seven. It was when they took Mum into hospital. She'd only another two years to go and she was in a dreadful state, mentally and physically —presenile dementia. I'd struggled on as long as I could. Then I collapsed.'

Armstrong made sympathetic noises.

'Best thing that happened to me. Laid my burdens on the Lord and He changed my whole life. The hospital place turned up for Mum and I got in touch with Cheryl and Martin.'

'Was your sister back working at the Foxwillow Arms?' Baxter asked.

'No. Place had closed down by then. There had been some sort of scandal. Drugs, I think. But it was all hushed up. Cheryl was temping and taking secretarial classes at the Tech—she'd picked up a few O-levels at school. Then about four years ago she got a job in a Cambridge book-shop. It's in Pepper Street—run by a French couple called Poulenc. And there she stayed. Surprised me really. Cheryl was a clever girl but not by any means the bookish type.'

'Did you see a good deal of her over these last six years?'

'No. She hadn't much time for me. But I saw a lot of Martin, especially when he was younger. Used to be scared of his own shadow, you know. But they helped him greatly at the clinic. And at the community college. He's a different boy . . .'

'I'm sure you helped too, Miss Taylor,' Armstrong mur-mured.

'Are you, Inspector?' The abruptness unsettled him.

'By the way,' Baxter asked, 'did you know your sister would be going to the clinic yesterday evening?'

'Yes,' Freda replied without hesitation or obvious embar-rassment. 'I rang Cheryl before supper—about six. To find out if Martin would be coming over on Sunday. She told me then. Made it an excuse for getting off the 'phone in a hurry.'

'And how did you spend yesterday evening?' The Chief Inspector contemplated her bandaged left wrist.

'The usual sort of thing. Washed my supper dishes. Knitted for a couple of hours. Read my library book. Watched the news on the telly at ten. Then prayers and bed.'

'A good, sensible woman,' Armstrong observed as she closed her front door behind them. 'Not what you'd call a fanatic.'

No. But 'good' and 'sensible' were also inadequate descriptors. Baxter wondered whether Freda Taylor heard voices when she said her prayers. And what they told her.

The children's ward in Holtchester District Hospital had recently been repainted. On the mural behind the bed in the private cubicle a tabby cat contemplated an assortment of birds and butterflies with unfeline tolerance. Baxter was glad that Martin Hobbs didn't have to meet its tawny eyes as he checked through the boy's possessions and asked him to relive his experiences of the previous evening.

'How did you feel when you saw your mother reading that file?'

Martin looked away, his left hand playing with a scab on his right forearm. 'Dunno.'

'Come on, lad. We know you didn't kill her.'

But he'd wanted to, hadn't he? 'I felt angry. Mad angry.'

'Why?'

'There was stuff in that file that was private between me and Dr Denny. She'd no right to be reading what was private and laughing about it.' As though it mattered. As though anything mattered now.

'What did you do?'

'Went into the kitchen.' The scrambled eggs they had given him for breakfast were lying heavily in his stomach.

'Why the kitchen?'

'Dunno.'

'Try again.'

He looked up at the three irrelevant faces. The lined face of the older detective, the polished face of the younger, the long, loving face of his aunt.

'I wanted a knife. Only to frighten her. I just wanted to frighten her.' He began to weep.

'May I?' Freda Taylor produced a packet of paper hand-kerchiefs. Baxter nodded. She pushed a tissue into Martin's left palm, curling his fingers round it. 'Tell them the truth, lad. The truth shall set you free.'

'I've told them.'

'What happened next?' Baxter prompted gently.

'When I got the knife out of the cutlery drawer I heard a noise.'

'Where did it seem to be coming from?'

'From—oh, I forget his name—the man with the beard —the drama therapist. It was from his office.'

'What kind of noise?'

'Dunno. Suppose you'd call it a thud. And some scuffling.'

'What did you do?'

'Tried to put the knife back in the drawer. But it slipped. Made a helluva noise on the tiles. So I ran to the loo and locked myself in. I needed the loo.'

And now he needed to be sick, but he wouldn't. He'd take deep breaths, like Dr Denny had told him. And concentrate on the worst thing that could possibly happen. But it already had.

'Groundfloor plan, Bill?' Armstrong passed it over, point-ing out the boys' lavatory behind Peter Denny's office.

'How long did you stay in the loo?'

'Ten minutes maybe. I heard footsteps soon after I went in there. Then a squeak. Then everything went quiet. Thought it must have been Mrs Tomlinson come down to talk to Mum. But I hadn't heard anyone on the stairs.'

'This squeak. What direction did it come from?'

'Dunno. Could have been the waiting-room door, I suppose. Or the hall door. Couldn't be sure.'

Baxter nodded. 'What happened next?'

'I—I might be sick.'

'Get him a kidney-dish.'

Armstrong found one in the bedside cupboard and placed it on the bed within arm's reach. The boy seemed to draw reassurance from the gleaming metal.

'Want a break?' Baxter asked.

He shook his head. Better get it over. 'I went back into Dr Denny's room. The waiting-room light had been switched off. Everything was very quiet—at first. Then I heard the funny sound. A sort of moaning.'

'A man's voice or a woman's?'

'I couldn't be sure. But it definitely wasn't my mum's.'

'Go on.'

'I got very scared then, and the dark was suffocating me. I hate the dark—hate it more than anything. So I switched on the light in Dr Denny's room.'

'And then?'

'Then the moaning stopped and the thing rushed out at me. It knocked me down, so I only got one quick look. But I could see the striped face and the fangs and the big claws. I've been thinking about it ever since I woke up. I'm not lying and I'm not crazy. But it couldn't have been a real tiger, could it?'

'No,' said Baxter, 'I think it was a human being in fancy dress.' *Dressed to kill.* The phrase jangled nonsensically in his mind. Looking down at the drained face on the bed, he knew that he would take little rest until he had refashioned it into some sort of sense.

CHAPTER 5

At twenty to eight Baxter's Rover drew up outside a neat bungalow on the outskirts of Maryham, a large village on the Cambridgeshire side of Newmarket. Steve Hobbs emerged from a green Morris Minor in his car port. He was a pale, flabby man. The middle button of his uniform jacket was strained over his belly.

The detectives displayed their cards. 'Mr Hobbs? May we come in?' Baxter asked.

Hobbs consulted a watch on his tattooed wrist. Worry lines contracted his forehead. 'I have to clock in by eight. They come down hard on unpunctuality, unless you've a cast-iron excuse.'

'But you have, Mr Hobbs, you have,' Baxter insisted. 'Assisting the police in their inquiries. Doing your civic duty.'

'All right then. You'd better come inside.' Hobbs led them into a light, well-ordered living-room. A blonde woman was clearing away breakfast dishes from the table in the dining area. 'My wife Linda. Chief Inspector Baxter.'

She stood her ground, gripping a loaded tray.

'Sorry to be a nuisance, Mrs Hobbs. We'd like to have a chat with your husband. On his own, if you don't mind.'

It was clear from her expression that she minded quite a lot.

Hobbs managed a smile. 'It's all right, love. Run along. Would you ring the depot for me? Tell them I'll be there as soon as poss.'

With a regretful glance in the direction of the remaining dishes, Linda Hobbs left the room. They could hear her dialling on the hall telephone.

'Sorry about that.' Hobbs ushered the detectives towards

a pair of hide settees. 'The wife didn't mean to be rude. It's just that she doesn't like being caught on the hop. Can you tell me what this is in aid of?'

'Murder, Mr Hobbs.'

'Jesus Christ. Not the boy, is it? Not Martin?'

'No. Your son's all right. He's had a shock but he's getting over it. The victim was Mrs Cheryl Hobbs.'

The fat man shook his head, seemingly stunned. 'What a waste. What a bloody useless waste.'

A conventional response, but Baxter had an inkling he wasn't using the words conventionally. 'Murder always is.'

'Yes, yes, I suppose so.'

'When did you last see your former wife, Mr Hobbs?'

'Oh, I don't know. It's been a long time since I saw her to talk to—we hadn't anything to say to each other, Cheryl and me. But I caught sight of her every now and then in Cambridge when the bus was stuck in some goddam traffic jam.'

'In her lunch breaks?'

'Maybe, maybe not. Her bosses seemed to be pretty free and easy, from what her sister told me. Not like the Transport. Lucky for some, I'd say. But it wasn't, was it, poor cow?'

'When was the last time you saw her?'

'Tuesday or Wednesday of this week, I reckon. Couldn't be certain. But it was about eleven in the morning.'

'This was in Cambridge?'

'Yeah—she was going into a bank—the NatWest in Fort Street.'

'And where did you spend yesterday evening, Mr Hobbs?'

'Let's see. I was on early shift—got home around 3.20, worked on the car till about six. Then I was in the bath for a good half-hour. I'm a mechanic by trade, you see. Still like tinkering about with engines when I get a chance. But Linda can't stand mess. Won't let me near the supper table with dirt under my nails.'

'What time did you eat?'

'Sometime around seven—I couldn't be sure. You'd better ask Linda.'

'And then what?'

'Wasn't much of a night for going out, was it? We watched telly. The science programme on ITV. Mostly astronomy this week—a bit above my head. Then the BBC1 News and the new thriller serial. We turned in around eleven.'

'Thank you. Can you remember when you last talked to your ex-wife, Mr Hobbs?'

'Oh, yes. Three years ago, it was, nearly to the day. Early October. Six months after I moved back into the area.'

'You seem pretty definite this time.'

Hobbs's hands tightened on his broad thighs. 'Not likely to forget. We had one helluva row.'

'What about?'

'Martin. Naïve of me, I suppose, but I thought I'd done all the right things. Moved back into the area. Settled my debts. Got myself a wife who liked kids. A steady job with a little extra business on the side. So I'd demanded my legal right of access to the boy twice a month.'

'But your ex-wife hadn't played ball?'

'By the letter of the law she had. Kid would be ready and waiting at his auntie's every other Sunday when I went to collect him. But he'd be scared stiff. Got sick in the car. Hardly opened his mouth the whole time he was here. Wouldn't eat—and the missus is a fabulous cook, you know. Cried himself to sleep when we tried a whole weekend. "Give it time," Linda said. She'd worked as a nanny, so I reckoned she ought to know.'

'But things hadn't improved?'

'Not really. He seemed to be coming round in the summer. Acted as if he was enjoying himself sometimes on the days we went swimming or fishing. But you can keep your distance in the river or the pool. I reckon he was happy there in spite of me. Then his new term started—he was at primary school then—and things went back to square one.'

'Any idea what was behind his attitude?'

'Kid wouldn't utter when I challenged him. But I came to the conclusion that Cheryl had been filling his head with lies about me. Deliberately scaring him off.'

'So you had it out with her in October?'

'Tried to, but she wouldn't listen. Said she'd told Martin the truth about me—no more, no less. If he didn't care for my company that just showed his good taste. And if I went on pressing for access I'd probably drive him round the bend. She said his headmistress had referred him for Child Guidance.' Hobbs blew his nose. 'Not a nice thing, that. To be told you're sending your kid off his head.'

'And you haven't spoken to your ex-wife since that meeting? Quite sure?'

'No point, was there? I saw the psychiatrist at the clinic soon after. He agreed that Cheryl might have rubbished me to the lad. If so, the social worker would try to get her to see she was acting against the boy's interests. But he couldn't promise she'd come round. In the meantime I'd better not push my claim. Cheryl would have grounds for an appeal to the court if compulsory contact was shown to be affecting the kid's mental health.'

'How did you feel about that?'

'Bloody awful. Went on the booze for a couple of weeks. Don't know how Linda put up with me. It was rough for her too. She's fond of kids and Martin was the only son I could give her. Had the op, you see.'

'Did you abandon all attempts at contact with the boy?'

'Reckoned I'd no alternative. I'd park outside the school grounds sometimes to catch a glimpse of him. It was easier when he moved up to the Community College—there's a longer frontage. And I'd pop into his auntie's—Freda Taylor's—to hear the latest news about him. She'd pass me on the odd snapshot.' He pulled out a wallet stuffed with more photographs than banknotes or credit cards.

Baxter inspected them politely. In the earlier photographs Martin was mostly on his own, or with Cheryl. In the more recent he sometimes appeared with a group of schoolchildren in a gymnasium, swimming pool or outdoors setting.

'Very nice.' He passed back the photographs. 'I understand Miss Taylor told you of her sister's plans to remarry. What did you make of that?'

'Didn't know what to think.' Hobbs contemplated a glass menagerie on the coffee-table. 'Wasn't too happy about the idea of Martin being carted off to Town—Freda seemed to think Cheryl's bloke was a Londoner. But I'd up sticks again to be near the boy if I had to. Reckoned this flash new husband mightn't have much time for another man's kid. I might even stand a better chance of access.'

'Better still as things are now, don't you think?' Armstrong's Ulster drawl twanged like a crossbow.

The fat man flushed. 'With Cheryl out of the way? I won't say I've never thought of that, for I did. But, other considerations apart, the lad would never have forgiven me if it had come out.'

'I dare say not, Mr Hobbs.' Baxter rose. 'That will be all for the present. Thank you for your help.'

'Tricky one, isn't it?' he mused, unwrapping a soda mint as Armstrong adjusted his seat-belt. 'Hard to believe that an emotional guy like Hobbs would play a waiting game for three whole years. But if not, what kind of a game was he up to?'

'I'll work on it.' Bill smiled the smile of a man with perfect digestion. 'Just give me time.'

But as that commodity was in short supply, Baxter decided to part company with his senior subordinate. Delegation had never come easily to him, but over the last decade he had learnt to accept its necessity. And because his instinct was to stay close to the habitual terrain of his victim, he called at the police station in Cambridge to telephone a request for Sergeant Short to join him at the City Guildhall. Armstrong he despatched in a police car to Holtchester Child Guidance Clinic.

A placard announcing the monthly book sale stood outside the nondescript building, but there were still twenty minutes to go before the ten o'clock opening time. There was an air of mild confusion in the blue and gilt interior as dealers identified their stalls, greeted old acquaintances and unpacked their crates. A typed list guided the detectives to the Poulencs in an out-of-the-way corner of the hall. Madame, a birdlike, blue-rinsed woman in her sixties, was arranging a meagre collection of books on folding shelves. An older man sat near her, strapped into a wheelchair. As the policemen approached they could see the tetchiness of his well-manicured hands.

Baxter showed the woman his card, and murmured the conventional request for an interview.

'A few minutes! I'm afraid that is more than we can spare at the moment, Chief Inspector. We've only just arrived, and, as you see, my husband is incapacitated. Something has happened to prevent my assistant . . .'

'Exactly, Madame. I'm afraid something very serious has happened to Mrs Hobbs. That's why Sergeant Short and I require your help.'

The woman's right ringed hand flew to her throat. For a fraction of a second the face that stared back at Baxter bore the hallmarks of terror. Then it settled into an expression of well-bred concern. Mme Poulenc took her husband's hand and bent over him.

'It's Cheryl, *mon chou*. She's had some sort of accident. I think in the circumstances . . .'

The old man raised clouded eyes. 'You must forgive Marie. Sometimes she forgets that I'm not mentally incapacitated—yet. We are both very fond of Cheryl: she has been like a daughter to us. If something serious has happened it would be kind to put us out of her misery.'

'She is out of hers, if that is any consolation.'

The old man shook his head. '"Whom the gods love,"
they say. But that doesn't help either.' He began to weep.

His wife shot him a look of concern. 'Shall we pack
up, Jean-Claude? I don't think I can face customers
today. Besides, the officers might prefer to talk to us in
private.'

Some late arrivals were setting out their stock on an
adjacent stall.

'Of course. I should be glad if someone could help my
wife with the fetching and carrying. As you see, I'm not
much use for anything . . .'

'A pleasure.' And something of an education. While
Madame was retrieving her car from the park and Short
was repacking crates under M. Poulenc's supervision,
Baxter read the prices on several dozen flyleaves and was
mildly shocked. He had a generalized interest in antiques,
but his expertise lay with old furniture. He didn't begrudge
a few hundred for fine carving or an eighteenth-century
patina, but he found it hard to sympathize with those who
valued books by their covers.

The detectives waited in Baxter's car outside the bookshop in Pepper Street. Mme Poulenc had refused the offer
of Short's company, insisting that she could easily unpack
the books at her leisure. She had announced her intention
of driving to the back entrance, which had been enlarged to
provide wheelchair access and parking space for one vehicle,
and had asked that they should park in front of the shop.
Pepper Street, a narrow thoroughfare off East Road, was an
unpromising location for a specialist bookshop. Few tourists
would have wandered that way and the nearest University
college was a mile distant. Several buildings in the dingy
street had boarded windows and For Sale notices. The
only operational businesses in addition to the bookshop
were a barber's shop, a timber merchant's yard and a

shabby garage. Sounds of banging and drilling could be heard from this last, which was located almost opposite the bookshop.

The policemen waited for two or three minutes before Marie Poulenc opened the door of the shop and beckoned them inside with apologies for the delay. 'I had to make my husband comfortable. It was the shock. You understand, gentlemen . . .'

They followed her through the dark shop into a small room with tasselled curtains. Except for a roll-top desk, it might have been the habitat of an old Parisian concierge. On a plush-covered table there stood a cut-glass decanter and four sherry glasses.

'You'll join us, gentlemen?' Jean-Claude spoke from his wheel chair in the corner.

Baxter accepted a teaspoonful of sherry to wash down another antacid tablet and Short declined.

'How can we help you?' their host asked.

Not much, it seemed. According to her employers, Cheryl Hobbs had kept herself very much to herself. A desirable trait, in Marie's opinion.

'It was a bond between us, I suppose. This is our home now, as well as our business. And living *en famille* with a chatterbox can be very trying.'

'What were Mrs Hobbs's responsibilities?' Baxter asked, turning to Jean-Claude.

'Pricing and repricing—to my dictation. Cataloguing, shelving, dusting, helping with the accounts. A little typing. Show them, Marie!' Obedient to his gesture, his wife unlocked and opened the roll-top desk. 'Thanks to our poor Cheryl, you will find everything in order.'

'I daresay, sir.' Baxter made a brief visual scan of the neatly clipped stacks of paper. 'Accountancy's a bit beyond me, I'm afraid. She did the typing at home. I believe?'

'By choice. We were flexible, you see. When Cheryl went up to London on business for us she was free to visit her friends. And in return she did a little typing for us at home in her free time.'

'And she took work home with her last Wednesday evening?'

Jean-Claude nodded. 'The price lists for the Book Fair.'

'A big job?'

'No. The typing was routine for Cheryl. The hard work came beforehand. Deciding which books to show, which prices to revise.'

'Anything strange about Cheryl's behaviour when she left the shop on Wednesday evening?'

Both his informants shook their heads.

'Did she say anything to either of you about her plans for remarriage?'

'Absolutely not.' It was Marie who replied. 'We had considered the possibility, Jean-Claude and I. Wondered if she would marry one of her London friends.'

'But she said nothing?'

'She wouldn't have, if it wasn't settled,' Marie insisted. 'She kept her private life very much to herself. For example, she hardly ever spoke about her son, although she told us of him when we first employed her.'

'How much did you pay her?'

Marie answered quickly: 'Eighty pounds a week before tax. With her expenses.'

'It was all we could afford,' Jean-Claude added.

Not much. A girl with Cheryl's looks and qualifications could have earned more in Cambridge. And found herself a livelier work environment. So why hadn't she? Baxter brooded over the anomaly as he took his leave.

The sun struggled with cloud as they drove off and shone in full brilliance as they passed the Backs. This was how Cambridge ought to look, Baxter reflected, watching the creamy stone buildings appear and disappear behind their screen of autumn foliage. How he had imagined it as a child when he had first read Frances Cornford's verses:

Down in the town off the bridges and the grass
They are sweeping up the leaves to let the people pass.
Sweeping up the old leaves, golden-reds and browns,
Whilst the men go to lecture with the wind in their
   gowns.

'Men!' his eight-year-old daughter had protested, when
she had first stumbled on the lines. 'Girls go to lectures too,
don't they? Girls can wear gowns.' He doubted very much
if academic dress was in vogue at the plate-glass university
of Emma's choice. It had been a rarity in his own redbrick
days.

A marmalade cat rose from the doorstep to greet them as
the car drew up outside the Newnham cottage of Andrew
and Jane Gordon. The house, like most of its neighbours,
seemed well cared for. The brass knocker gleamed on a
white painted door. Dwarf chrysanthemums glowed in the
window-boxes. A smell of newly baked bread wafted out as
Jane Gordon answered Short's rap, looking every inch an
Earth Mother despite her guernsey sweater and floury
dungarees.

'Police. Good Lord! Has my past been catching up with
me?' she asked with a jocularity she must have acquired as
an overweight teenager.

'I hope not. I very much hope not,' Baxter replied gravely.
'May we come in?'

'My husband's out, I'm afraid.'

'Don't worry, Mrs Gordon. It's you we'd like to speak to,
in the first instance.'

The cat followed them into a pleasant little dining-room
and made for the window-seat. The room was furnished to
Baxter's conventional taste. The wheelback chairs looked
original and the dresser held an attractive mixture of blue-
and-white porcelain and treen.

'Perhaps someone from the Child Guidance Clinic has
already been in touch?' he asked.

'No. Why?' Jane sat down on the window-seat, the men on dining-chairs.

'There's been a murder on the premises.'

'Not a child?' Her fingers reached for the cat's warm fur.

'A parent. Mrs Cheryl Hobbs.'

Jane gasped softly, her face flooding with colour.

'Did you know her?'

'Only by sight. I saw her with Martin in the clinic waiting-room on a couple of occasions.'

'You had dealings with the boy?'

'Not really. Dr Denny asked me to give him some educational attainment tests before treatment was terminated. And to check up on his progress and adjustment with his teachers. And I've recently done a follow-up visit to the school at Mrs Tomlinson's request.'

'But you didn't discuss any of your findings with the boy's mother. Isn't that unusual?'

'No. I should have done if I'd been dealing with the case single-handed. But two other team members were involved and its against the principles of human resources therapy to confront parents with too many different professionals.'

'Did you know Cheryl Hobbs would be in the clinic yesterday evening?'

'Yes—to use the typewriter.' No hesitation there. 'Luke Mason told me at lunchtime that he'd invited her.'

'What did you make of that?'

'I was a bit surprised. Hilde wouldn't have approved. Role confusion and all that. HRT social workers aren't supposed to be general purpose problem-solvers. And if Martin had still been in treatment I'd have been inclined to agree. But to all intents and purposes the case was closed. So why not?'

'Cheryl Hobbs was reading Martin's clinic file when she died.'

'Oh God. Patients' records are sacrosanct. Hilde will go berserk when she finds out.'

'She has and she didn't,' Baxter replied crisply. 'Any idea why someone might kill to read those casenotes? Or to prevent Cheryl Hobbs from talking about them?'

Jane shook her head, pale now. Reading the shadows beneath her candid blue eyes, Baxter realized for the first time that she was pregnant. 'No names, no pack drill in those notes, as far as I remember. Cheryl was canny.'

But Luke Mason wasn't, sod him.

'Did you tell anyone else about Mrs Hobbs going to the clinic yesterday evening?'

'I may have told my husband over supper—I can't remember. Beaujolais loosens my tongue and last night we were celebrating.'

'A baby?'

'Really, Chief Inspector.' A wry smile. 'You're in the wrong profession, aren't you?' She pulled the cat onto her lap and began to stroke it.

'I'd be glad to know how you spent yesterday evening. What time was supper.'

'Sevenish. We like to eat early.'

'Did you and your husband spend the evening together?'

She shook her head. 'Unfortunately, no. We stoked up with black coffee and got back to work in our studies.'

'Work?'

'I was checking some stats on my computer and Andy was examining a master's thesis. On Pascal, I think. He could fill you in on the details, if necessary.'

'Good. How long did you work?'

'About an hour in my case. I'm more of a lark than an owl at the best of times. And the coffee was fighting a losing battle with the Beaujolais.'

'And then?'

'Then the ten o'clock news headlines. A shower and bed.'

'Go on.'

Her eyes flickered but there was no pause in the slow, rhythmical stroking movement of her strong right hand. 'Andy woke me when he came to bed. At one or two o'clock, I think—his usual sort of time.'

'Uh-huh?'

'I went to the loo and came back and we made love. Would you like a diagram, Chief Inspector, or will a verbal description suffice?'

Short flinched empathetically as his chief took the full force of the boomerang.

'There is really no necessity . . .' Baxter began.

'No, no. Of course there isn't.' Jane blew her nose. 'Sorry about that. I get a bit uptight these days. Hormones, I suppose.'

'Beyond my expertise, I'm afraid. You've been very patient.' He stood up and she followed his example, still clutching the cat. 'You might like to have this letter, by the way. I shall need the envelope back.' He handed her the unopened letter bearing the crest of the University Hospital which they had found in Eileen Lethbridge's desk drawer. 'By the way, do you normally have your private correspondence sent to the clinic?'

She looked a little uneasy. 'Appointment letters are hardly private if they're churned out by computers. As you see, they couldn't even get my name right on the address label. But all the same, I don't propose to discuss the contents with you. On principle.'

'And I didn't ask you. On the same principle. But I should like to know if you normally receive private mail at the clinic.' He smiled ingratiatingly.

'Not now. I used my work address temporarily when we were moving house about eighteen months ago. There was a hitch and we had to spend a couple of months in rented rooms. We were worried about post going astray. I notified most people when we moved in here, but one tends to overlook institutional correspondents.'

And yet she had struck him as a highly organized woman.

'Where does your husband generally work?'

'It varies. At home in the evenings and weekends. Mostly in college during office hours, but sometimes in the French Department or in the University Library. He's hellishly busy just at present. Will you really have to see him?'

'Sooner or later.' It would be interesting to know where Andrew Gordon bought his books. But for the present Baxter had other priorities.

'Where next?' Colin Short asked, with the keenness of a young officer who was determined to hold his place in the fast promotion stream against all comers.

'Headquarters.' Baxter let himself into his car and released the catch on the front passenger door. 'Time I caught up with my reading.' With a considerable effort Short managed to conceal his disappointment and his curiosity.

CHAPTER 6

Baxter selected the pathologist's report from the array of papers on his desk.

'Manual strangulation from behind by a right-handed assailant.' Or a left-hander with a wrist injury? 'Deceased was seated at the time of the attack . . . no evidence of sexual assault at the time of attack but indications of sexual intercourse some 4½ to 5 hours beforehand.'

He read and reread the notes from the lab. They'd found no traces of blood other than Cheryl's. The gloved prints on her neck matched those on her son's clinic file and the outside door of Peter Denny's room. Looked as though the break-in had been a plastic card job—that was the only door in the building with a Yale lock. Despite the rain there were a few identifiable footprints. Mass-produced rubber soled boots, they reckoned. Size 10. To judge by their direction, the wearer had left by the side entrance from which he or she had presumably entered. There were plenty of other fingerprints from the waiting-room, of course, and the signs of halfhearted dusting one expected of a public building. And a scrap of black cotton on the treasury tag fastening the boy's file that matched a fibre from the dead woman's neck.

Knowing what you don't know is the beginning of wisdom, Baxter told himself as he picked up his telephone and dialled a London number.

'Bought any good books recently, Louie?'

'I should be so lucky, mate. You're talking to one of the world's workers. Forgotten the meaning of the word, I expect, up in that ivory tower of yours!'

'This *is* work, Lou. Work with a capital W in the eyes of my Chief. Your facsimile machine working?' Baxter had not as yet fully assimilated the concept of document transmission. 'Good. There's a catalogue coming over. Six sheets. French titles, mostly—ancient and modern. I need a specialist opinion.'

'On what?'

'Content. Is this run-of-the-mill stuff or are there some collectors' items? And prices. Low, medium or cheeky? Think you can deliver?'

'Louie always delivers.' Baxter could visualize his ex-colleague's look of injured pride without benefit of digital electronics. 'Given a reasonable deadline. Monday good enough?'

'Not really. I need to know by tomorrow evening. But don't bother to cross the "t's". Rough impressions will do, as long as they come from an expert.'

'Nothing but the best, mate. Leave it to Lou.'

And so he would. On the way back from the document

transceiver he collected a sandwich lunch from the cafeteria and took it to his desk.

Martin Hobbs's clinic file contained documents of four types: letters, diagnostic reports, treatment notes and a list of dates of attendance at the clinic by the boy and his mother. The notes on treatment were colour coded—yellow for the psychiatrist's, green for the social worker's. And the back pocket of the folder contained half a dozen spare sheets of bank in each colour. Both sets of casenotes were handwritten—Hilde Tomlinson's in black ink and firm, regular style and Peter Denny's in ballpoint scribble. Luckily, Hilde was by far the more verbose of the two. Baxter took a bite of Caerphilly, celery and wholemeal bread, and plunged into his task. He had read five pages when the telephone rang. It was Bill Armstrong from the clinic.

'Can you come over soonish? Natives getting restless.'

'Ten minutes.' Baxter sighed, munching his sandwiches with all deliberate speed between sips of milky coffee. He'd wanted thinking time as much as reading time. But Bill wouldn't have called him out on a fool's errand. Flexibility was one of the names of the game, he reminded himself, as he warned the incidents room of his departure before taking the lift for the underground car park.

Five minutes later Armstrong met him in the hall of the clinic, a tall, bearded man at his side. Luke Mason sat slumped on a hard chair a few yards away. A constable stood at the foot of the stairs.

'Mr Aiken's the drama therapist,' Armstrong explained, ushering the bearded man into the waiting-room ahead of his senior officer. 'He's an urgent appointment.' He closed the door behind them.

'Session at a centre for the mentally handicapped.' Aiken elaborated. 'Never let them down yet. Reliability's the only virtue some of them cotton on to, poor bastards.'

'Mr Aiken's been very helpful. Given us a good description of a tiger costume that's gone missing from his office.'

'Cast-iron alibi, too,' Jos Aiken cut in. 'Which is more to the point, isn't it? Panto rehearsal at my drama club last night—seven to nine-thirty. Good turn-out. The Inspector's got a dozen names to be going on with.'

'Very well, then. We won't hold you back. Many thanks, Mr Aiken.' Baxter held open the waiting-room door, hoping the therapist could not sense the relief with which he was ridding himself of his presence. Aiken reminded him painfully of the facilitator at some group therapy sessions in which he had been required to engage in the course of in-service training. And public soul-scraping was without doubt his least favourite activity. 'About this costume.'

'He was pretty precise. Nothing realistic, he said. Just a three-piece. Loose, long-sleeved gown, reaching to the knees of an average adult. Hood with a tiger mask. Mitts with claws. Says a kid in his therapy group was wearing the outfit in the clinic yesterday afternoon. Sure it was put back in one of the cardboard boxes in his office at the end of the session.'

'Could Martin Hobbs have seen the costume before last night?'

'Aiken doesn't think so. Not unless he made a habit of prowling round the place. And Eileen Lethbridge would soon have put paid to that. Aiken never had the lad in treatment and he kept his bunch inside the playroom when they were dressed up. Besides, Denny's individual treatment sessions were nearly always held outside drama therapy hours. Denny couldn't stand the noise, it seems.'

'Mmm. Coming together, isn't it?'

'Is it?'

'Murderer enters by the side door of Peter Denny's office.'

'Why? When?'

'Discretion. If he—or she—hadn't come with criminal intent the sight of Luke's fond farewell might well have lit the fuse.'

'So X lurked about in the alley till Mason had left?'

'I'd guess. Maybe he spotted the light in Hilde's room, maybe not.'

'What then?'

'Must have made a quiet job of the break-in, but Cheryl's typing would have made a fair din. Reckon X hung around a bit in Denny's room, watching and waiting. But I fancy it wasn't long before Cheryl's curiosity about the files got the better of her. In all probability the murderer saw—and heard—much the same as Martin did a few minutes later.'

'And it sent him scuttling off into the drama therapist's room?'

'Could be. Probably wanted time to come to terms with the situation—to work out the next step. Especially if Hilde Tomlinson chose that moment to visit the loo.'

'X could have gone into the staff kitchen.'

'Where Cheryl or Hilde—assuming X wasn't Hilde— might so easily have gone to make a cuppa? Hardly. Jos Aiken's room offered a safer hiding-place and—as X may or may not have known beforehand—a useful range of disguises.'

'Then the kid made his entry. Think X would have heard that?'

'Probably not. But the chances are that he—or she— heard Martin coming downstairs and reopening the squeaking door into the psychiatrist's room which X had closed behind him. If the kid's report of scuffling noises is correct, X was already getting into his fancy dress when Martin came into the kitchen.'

'And whatever else X did or didn't hear, he can't have missed the clatter of the knife on the tiled floor.'

'Or the noise of the kid rushing off to the loo. It would be nice to find that tiger costume.' Baxter sounded despondent.

'Think we will?'

'Maybe. X was a clever enough cuss to wipe off most of

his fingerprints at the scene. I doubt if he'd leave the thing as a free gift to the forensic boys. On the other hand, he may not have had a chance to burn or bury it. It's probably in a cupboard or a car boot somewhere. Possibly awaiting future use.'

'God.' Armstrong grimaced. 'Do you really believe that?'

'I've no reason. It was just a hunch. One of those bloody depressing hunches. Cheer me up.'

'We've got a record of the Hobbs's clinic attendance. Photocopies of the relevant pages from the appointments diaries.'

'Well done.' Baxter told himself he would have thought of it—sooner or later. But later might have been too late. 'Denny didn't object?'

'Not as long as the names of other clients were masked out. Eileen Lethbridge made a thorough job of that. Gave her something to do, I suppose. Strikes me as a woman who likes to be busy.'

'No doubt. Anything else I ought to know about?'

'Come next door. Denny's upstairs.' Armstrong led the way from the waiting-room through the communicating door into the Medical Director's office. Using a pencil, he eased open the unlocked door of a wall cupboard to reveal a second metal cabinet. With all the delicacy of a priest approaching a tabernacle he opened this inner container to reveal a small collection of labelled bottles, tubes and ampoules.

The Chief Inspector squinted at the labels. 'Anti-convulsants, anti-histamine, painkillers. Nothing to get excited about, if they are what they seem. Daresay they come in handy for emergencies.'

'So Dr Denny tells me. He doesn't go in much for drugs. But they get the odd attack of migraine, asthma and epilepsy on the premises, and he likes to deal with emergencies promptly if he's on the spot.'

'Have we any reason to believe there's more to it?'

'Probably not. Denny's a bit fidgety . . .'

'Well, he's under stress. Murder on the premises and the loss of his London job. Anyone else have a key?'

'He says not. Keeps a record of stock and drugs dispensed.' Armstrong indicated a small notebook on the psychiatrist's desk. 'According to this, he gave a couple of codeine tablets to an adolescent patient at 11.10 yesterday morning. She'd complained to Eileen Lethbridge of severe menstrual pains.'

'Fair enough. Fingerprints?'

'Only his, they think, on the handles. Haven't touched the contents till you had a look. Warned him that we'd probably want to take them away for analysis.'

'Good man. I'd better make a courtesy call. Denny and Hilde Tomlinson both upstairs?'

'In her office. They've had some food brought in from the pub. Eileen Lethbridge's up there too.'

'Do I need to talk to her?'

'Shouldn't advise it. She's liable to go on a bit about being kept out of "her" waiting-room. Murder's just third-degree mess in her estimation.'

'And what was she up to yesterday evening?'

'Having supper with her living-in boyfriend. And her sister rang up around eight. Sister's liable to go on a bit too, it seems.'

Baxter was relieved to find Eileen relatively subdued when he entered Hilde Tomlinson's office. The sudden silence and the quantity of uneaten food suggested that strategy planning had been in progress. He addressed the trio from the doorway:

'Thank you all for your cooperation. There's no reason to detain you further as far as we're concerned. We're clearing up downstairs.'

'The telephone . . .' Eileen Lethbridge protested. 'Someone is always here to cover during clinic hours.'

'Switch it through as you go out, Eileen,' Hilde told her. 'Peter and I will be here until five.'

'If you're quite sure . . . I could certainly do with the afternoon off.' She was already wriggling into her aquamarine showerproof. 'Let's hope things get back to normal by Monday.'

'Rather a tall order, Chief Inspector.' Peter Denny looked tired but confident. Like a man who had plummeted the depths and resurfaced glad to be alive. Baxter felt sure that he had broken his bad news to his wife.

'I daresay Eileen will settle for a tidy waiting-room,' Hilde observed. 'She's had plenty of practice here in skating over unpleasant realities.'

'While the professionals keep on chipping.'

She laughed. '*Touché*, Chief Inspector. I prefer to think we sit around until the ice melts.'

'Mrs Lethbridge has worked here for five years, I understand. Has her work proved satisfactory?'

'Certainly,' Denny replied. 'She knows her limitations and operates within them. She's paid to keep the system flowing and she does just that—ten times better than some psycho-therapist *manqué*.'

'I see. Now will you both please accept my apologies for keeping you cooped up here.'

'Of course.' So Hilde could be gracious when she chose. 'Dr Denny and I have plenty to discuss. Besides, there'll be a barrage of inquiries from anxious parents once people get their hands on the local papers—appeals for professional reassurance. And we can't pass the buck.'

The telephone rang as if on cue, but the call was for Baxter and detained him for less than a minute.

'Anything more we can do for you?' Peter Denny asked.

'I'd like to borrow this if I may. As background reading.' Baxter indicated the symposium on human resources therapy.

'Of course.' Denny rose. 'And apologies if I seemed obsessed with private woes last night. You do realize that Mrs Tomlinson and I are desperately anxious to see this business cleared up—at whatever cost. 'If we can be of any further help . . .'

'I shan't hesitate to approach you.'

But for the present Baxter's business was with Luke Mason. For the second time he interviewed the young man in the playroom, with Armstrong in attendance.

'Just got some news for you—news to Inspector Armstrong as well. You'll be pleased to hear, Bill, that we've found a second witness to support Mr Mason's alibi.'

'Pleased? Him?' Mason snarled. 'Is this some kind of fuzzy joke?'

'Not at all. My colleague believed your story.'

'And you didn't?'

'I suspended judgement. Sexual frustration is a powerful motive and Cheryl Hobbs was a desirable woman.'

'For Christ's sake. Who did the needful?'

'Landlord of the Blue Waggon—you heard about that one, Bill. And Mrs Harper-Dean.'

'Do I know Mrs Harper-Dean?'

'Shouldn't think so. She's a gentlewoman in reduced circumstances, I gather, with strong views on multiple tenancy. Owns a property in Wordsworth Square, and complains regularly about the lifestyle of occupants of neighbouring bedsitters.'

'She reported the noise from my bike engine?'

'Not once but twice. With a ten-minute interval between calls. Lads were otherwise engaged the first time, and you were away by the time they made it.'

Luke giggled. 'I suppose I should write her a bread-and-butter letter. "Dear Mrs Harper-Dean." She'd hate that, wouldn't she? To know she'd got a public nuisance off the hook.'

'She mightn't be sorry to accelerate your departure from Holtchester. I take it you'll be keen to get back to college.'

'Not any more. I've given up that idea.'

'On Mrs Tomlinson's recommendation?'

'No. To give her her due, Hilde bent over backwards to
be fair. Said I'd made an error of judgement, but so had
many beginners. No one could have predicted the conse-
quences. She recommended a second fieldwork placement
in the personal services sector during the Easter vac.'

'But you're turning down the option. Not from self-pity,
I hope.' From the corner of his eye, Baxter could see Armstrong flicking the rubber band that bound his notepad.

'No, from self-knowledge. Community work always was
a means to an end for me. Jane Gordon hinted as much to
me yesterday and she was right. I fancied myself as a
politician—still do. Community work looked like a good
way of getting to understand the problems of the underdogs,
learning to speak their language.'

'Not any longer?'

Luke Mason shook his head.

'Human resources therapy is a farce as far as I'm concerned and I didn't let myself get involved emotionally with
any of Hilde's cases. Until Cheryl. I haven't got over Cheryl
and I never will. But her pain was over so quickly compared
with thousands'. The thousands a community worker's supposed to relate to. Their pain would tear me apart. Does
that sound crazy?'

'No. But a course of training might make you feel dif-
ferently.'

'Professional mystique and all that—I dare say you're
right. Oh I need a role just as much as the social workers
do. But I want one that's as clearly understood by my clients
as myself. None of this Little friend of All the World kitsch
one minute and official freeze-out the next. Testing the
limits, they call it. I reckon the poor have better things to
do with their time.'

'So what's your solution?' For a second or two Baxter felt
as though he was interrogating himself when twenty.

'Dunno. Might try street-sweeping—or the law. My girlfriend would probably find that one hard to take. If she's still my girlfriend.'

'You'll be heading North?' Baxter asked, recalling the postcard from the peace camp.

'If you've finished with me.'

'Just a couple of questions. Was Mrs Hobbs wearing nail polish when you visited her at home yesterday?'

'Yes—peachy stuff. On her fingers and toes. She had lovely feet.'

'I remember.' The slides from the path lab flickered in quick succession before the detective's inward eye. 'Was it chipped, this polish?'

'Not that I noticed.'

'Was she wearing perfume at that time?'

'No. Not when I saw her in her house. Doesn't make sense, does it?'

'It will. Sooner or later it will.'

'Any offers?' Baxter asked Armstrong when they were alone.

'I should say the nail varnish was there at lunchtime because she hadn't got round to cleaning it off. But she'd probably showered off yesterday's perfume that morning.'

'And later?'

'Maybe she cleaned off the varnish with a view to changing the colour, but didn't get round to it. Or maybe she had an afternoon date with someone who fancied the unspoilt country girl image.'

'And the perfume?'

'Could have been the time factor again. Scent's a lot quicker to apply than nail polish. Maybe it was for Luke Mason's benefit. She might have thought he was worth a little effort but not too much.'

'Or that he was in her pocket already?'

'Could be. Whichever way you look at it, Cheryl Hobbs seems to have been an easy lay.' Armstrong grimaced.

Chastity beat charity by a long head in his rank order of female virtues.

The scent of Joy was overlaid by stronger chemical odours as Freda Taylor contemplated the face of her dead sister.

'"The Lord giveth, the Lord taketh away." It's for the best, you know.'

Baxter growled, replacing the sheet, and leading the way back into the corridor.

'You're not a believer, Chief Inspector?'

'Beliefs are luxuries I can't afford at present,' he told her as he steered her towards the entrance of the pathology department.

Back in his office he indulged himself in another brand of luxury. Grappling with new ideas had always proved to be an effective anaesthetic. And he needed to dull the anger with which he recalled the body of Cheryl Hobbs. The long legs, the small, clumsily stabbed breasts. A curiously immature body for a woman in her thirties. But sacrificial victims were traditionally immature. He imagined the act of killing. The big hands tightening on the throat. The fumbling for the knife. The superfluous butchery. The killer's rush to escape. And the glimpse of the boy's frightened face—the reminder that real escape was impossible.

The scenes would play and replay in Baxter's imagination until they began to make sense. And he would not have it otherwise. But if he was to think clearly he needed to distance and diminish them. Willing himself to concentrate, he opened *Human Resources Therapy*. Luckily it was one of those academic texts which carried summary pages at the end of each chapter. Read on their own, these condensed overviews were hard going. But the psychological and sociological theory he had acquired at courses and conferences proved equal to the task.

Human resources therapy, Holtchester style—for the

phrase signified different concepts in different places—
boasted little that was novel in theory or technique. The text
rehashed Freudian principles in the jargon of well-known
American therapists of the sixties and seventies. What was
new—or purported to be—was a matter of management.
Denny, Tomlinson and their adherents championed the
teamwork approach to the treatment of emotional and be-
havioural disorders, especially in children. But the traditional therapeutic team of highly paid professionals was
under threat in a cold economic climate. Denny and Tomlinson proposed a flexible, cost-cutting approach. Parents,
teachers, brothers and sisters and other adults could be
roped in as support figures—even, under supervision, as
therapists. Child clients' personal skills could be more effectively tapped so that they could take a greater share of
responsibility for their own therapy.

All very plausible. Especially, no doubt, when backed up
by the detailed reports of cases treated on such principles,
which he could not spare time to read. And yet, and yet.
The system might reduce the numbers of established child
guidance professionals—psychiatrists, psychologists, social
workers, psychotherapists. But it enhanced rather than
diminished their prestige. They were involved in diagnosis,
in the selection of treatment teams, and as consultants to
lay therapists. As Baxter read the summary of summaries
that concluded the book he became convinced that human
resources therapy, for all its wisdom and liberality, was
essentially a rearguard action in defence of an endangered
species.

His half-hour had not been wasted. He might have
gleaned little of theoretical or practical value from the
textbook, but he had gained insight into the motivations of
its authors. Especially Hilde Tomlinson's. For as he returned to the Hobbs file he realized that the style of her
casenotes—taut and precise—was the style of the summaries in *Human Resources Therapy*. Peter Denny and the other

contributors had, he deduced, gone along for the ride and travelled hopefully. But Hilde, he was prepared to bet, had taken charge of the reins. And, in case of need, the whip.

To judge by the file record, Martin Hobbs's case had been well handled. Someone had once told Baxter that empathy, warmth and genuineness were the hallmarks of good counselling. All three were evident here in good measure. Peter Denny's scribbles revealed that for many months their sessions had been a source of pleasure to both of them. Hilde, who had encountered much stiffer opposition in her attempts to relate to Cheryl, showed understanding and remarkable honesty in her reporting of their exchanges.

Factually, the records supported Freda Taylor's evidence and contributed little that was new. Martin had talked of his fears—fears of his primary school teacher of the dark, of bullying in the playground, of abduction by his father. With the move to secondary school a clamming-up process began. There was less and less talk of feelings, more of external events. Martin described his new school activities —sometimes with enthusiasm and pride, but latterly more often in the stereotyped fashion of a response to an adult-assigned exercise.

Baxter looked at his watch. 3.30. Time to heave himself out of the NeoFreudian undergrowth into the hard light of fact. He compared the sequence of visits entered in the appointments diary with the dates quoted at the back of the file. They matched. He checked these dates against the dated casenotes, and found a discrepancy. He checked again. There could be no doubt. Cheryl Hobbs was reported to have visited the clinic on February 23 of the current year, but there was no record of the interview she presumably had with Hilde Tomlinson.

He took out a magnifying glass and examined the thread of the treasury tag. No scrap of paper to indicate a torn-out page. He placed the glass over the following entry, dated March 9. The content of the entry offered no clue to the puzzle, no

reference to an aborted meeting. But he derived a more positive result from an inspection of the impressions overlaying
and interspersing the ink. It was clear that Hilde Tomlinson
made use of the spare sheets enclosed in the file, and that she
used them as a pad. The number 23 could be discerned among
a jumble of other impressions near the top of the page. And
three or four lines down there was a clear imprint of a capital
P. Looking back through previous entries, Baxter concluded
that this letter in isolation was used as a frequent alternative
to the initials PD in reference to Dr Denny. With heightened
excitement he confirmed that the single capital appeared in
locations on the written pages which were quite incompatible
with the position of its impression on the entry for the ninth
of March. He felt confident that he had discovered evidence
of an incomplete entry for the 23rd of February, although he
lacked the tools to decipher its content.

Had the missing entry been removed from the file after
insertion or had it never been included? Baxter was inclined
to the latter hypothesis. He felt certain that Hilde Tomlinson
rarely botched a job. And on the few occasions when she
did she might well be chary of advertising her failure. On
the other hand, she had struck him as a fundamentally
honest person.

Forcing himself to postpone further speculation, he
drafted a second media release which disclosed the name of
the dead woman. Then he rang Armstrong, who had remained behind at the clinic.

'Just about to 'phone you, Dick. Nothing much doing
here. Shall I come over to the station?'

'How about knocking off for a couple of hours?'

'If you say so.'

'We've both had an early start. I was rather hoping you
and Colin Short might take a run out to the Ruffled Feathers
later on. It's hardly my scene.'

'Or Peter Denny's.'

'Precisely.'

CHAPTER 7

Frost glinted malignly on the lawn as the Baxters finished breakfast on Saturday.

'Good bonfire weather.' Sarah was already in her gardening overalls.

'Lucky for some,' Richard muttered, wishing he could deal as swiftly and confidently with the pile of rubbish that awaited him.

A bright sun mocked him as he drove to the station. And Armstrong, overtaking him in the corridor, exuded an optimism to which he did not pretend to respond.

'Well?' Baxter growled when they were inside his office.

'Ruffled any good feathers recently?'

'We've made a start. There were forty-three customers in the brasserie last night and a dozen in the main restaurant. Eighteen of the brasserie crowd owned up to being there on Thursday too. Ten of them remembered seeing a man fitting Denny's description, but no one except a waitress and the barman actually spoke to him. And nobody saw his car arrive.'

'So he may or may not have come from the direction of London. Hell. Anything odd about his appearance or behaviour?'

'Not that anyone reported. Said he wanted his steak medium rare. Passed the odd remark about the wet weather. Toddled into the main restaurant and spent most of his time doing a crossword. That was the height of it.'

'Did he talk to anyone who didn't reappear last night?'

'The witnesses say not. There were evidently three couples in the restaurant when Denny came through from the brasserie—one pair of elderly locals and two sets of trendy young marrieds. Waitress gave a good description so we can follow

them up. As far as she could see there was no interaction—
they all left before he did. Girl says he asked for his bill
about ten and paid it promptly. Stayed on for some minutes
longer—she's not sure how long.'

'Killing time?'

'That's what the manager thought. Pretty typical behaviour, he reckoned. Knew Denny by sight. Came here about
once a month. One odd thing, though.'

'Oh?'

'He sat at the window on Thursday evening. Not his usual
seat. And the window overlooks the car park.'

'Waiting for someone who didn't turn up? Could be.'

'Want us to work on it? It could cost a bob or two, and
it won't tell us where he was at the time of the murder.'

'Work on it. The Met aren't likely to strike oil in the King
Edward. Not the sort of pub where people take time to stand
and stare.'

'See you've had the second instalment from the forensic
lab.' Armstrong nodded towards the envelope that had
arrived in the courier post. 'Anything special?'

'Leafmould. Beech leafmould in Cheryl Hobbs's cycle
pannier matches traces from the bootprints on the carpet.'

'Well—well. Wouldn't have thought of the deceased as
an outdoor girl, would you?'

'But we don't know her, for Christ's sake,' Baxter
snapped. 'We're only beginning to know her.' A process
which should accelerate if they shifted their sights from the
place where Cheryl had died to the place where she had
lived.

'Nothing else?'

'Take a look at these.' Baxter passed over three sheets of
paper. The file entry for March 9 had been chemically
treated before photographic enlargement so that the impressions of earlier notes stood out more clearly than the
words in ink. 'It's the incomplete entry I'm interested in.
Make it out?'

Armstrong aligned the pages and read aloud:

'"Mrs H arrived late. No explanation when I commented on fact. She said attendance was now a complete waste of time for her and for Martin. I reminded her that on several occasions she had remarked on the boy's improvement. She agreed, but said he'd simply grown out of his problems. And she had never had any that I could understand. I should have sorted myself out before I started interfering with other people's lives. She knew all about P and me. P was nothing . . ." Nothing *what*, I wonder?'

'Nothing *but*, I should say. Nothing but something so unacceptable to Hilde that she couldn't bring herself to write it down. And my guess is that she isn't a lady who often leaves a job half done.'

'So we're going to pay a call on her?'

'I think so. But first . . . Hell's bells.' He reached for the ringing telephone.

'Incidents room, sir. We've a Mrs Wright on the outside line. Lives opposite the Hobbs's house. Bit of a madam, by the sound of her. Says her son Dave has something to report. Incident involving young Martin at the school. Want them brought in?'

'No—no, we'll call round.' More rubbish to be raked through. Sour-smelling rubbish, Baxter was prepared to bet. Might as well get it over with.

'Something to drink, gentlemen?' Shirley Wright's heavily ringed hand hovered near her cocktail cabinet. 'No? You'll pardon me if I indulge. Had one helluva rough night. Don't mind telling you.'

'Meantersay,' she went on, subsiding into a corner of a plush-covered settee. 'You worry about young lads getting mixed up with the wrong sort. Don't know what to do for the best sometimes, do you?'

Baxter's eyes skimmed from the heavy marshmallow face

to the diagonal stripe of her mauve and lemon tracksuit. She was a big woman, with shrewd dark eyes and full magenta lips. There was a close resemblance between her and her son, lolling now in an easy chair at the other end of the room, lids half-shut and head swaying to the rhythms from his headphones.

'Cigarettes?' They watched her fiddle with a gilt holder. 'Meantersay, my usual instinct's to keep my mouth shut at a time like this. Can't blame me, can you?'

The Chief Inspector grunted.

'Don't want to speak ill of the dead, do you? First thing I said to the old man when I saw last night's paper. Maybe she had it coming, I said. But who are we to judge? There but for the grace of God . . .'

'But you changed your mind,' Armstrong smiled encouragingly.

'When Dave told me about this business at the school.'

'What business at the school?' Baxter asked. The detectives had concentrated in their interrogation of Martin Hobbs on his experiences at the clinic.

'The boy will tell you. *Dave?*'

Her son switched off his walkman and pushed back his headphones with seeming reluctance.

'Well?' Baxter put his face into neutral.

'Martin Hobbs got upset over something I said Thursday evening. 'Spect he's told you.'

'You tell me.'

'Not much to tell.'

'Try.'

'Well, he was buying this pair of earrings for his mum, see. From Susie Foster. Some of the girls make jewellery at the Centre. Susie said he'd bought her another pair last summer, but she'd lost them. Bit careless, I reckoned.'

'Really?'

'Yeah, really.' Dave scratched his left ankle.

'And you said so?'

The boy wriggled. 'Yeah—had Martin on a bit. No harm intended.'

'What else did you say?'

'Nothing that I remember.' Dave scratched harder, avoiding eye contact. 'If I did, it was just for a laugh. But the kid seemed to get really upset. Ran off as if there was something chasing him.'

A tiger, Baxter thought. *Tiger, tiger, burning bright.*

'What did you do then?'

Dave shrugged. 'Nothing, really. Just went on talking to Susie.'

'And that's God's truth, Inspector,' his mother added. 'No one can tell you my son's not honest, whatever else they may say against him. He's always been a big lad for his age . . .'

'Oh, Ma, for Chrissake . . .'

'And maybe he was inclined to throw his weight around when he was at the primary. But he was never half as bad as his teachers made out. That Martin Hobbs is a bundle of nerves, if you ask me. And no wonder with the life he's led.'

'How long have you and Mrs Hobbs been neighbours?'

'Seven or eight years. Cheryl moved to the estate a few months after she and Steve split up. But I'd known her long before that. Ever since we worked at the Foxwillow Arms.'

'So you were pretty close.'

Shirley Wright laughed. 'Anything but.' Her face settled into an expression of wounded virtue. 'Not my doing, mind. I was ready to be the good neighbour for old times' sake. But she didn't want it that way. Toffee-nosed little bitch was Cheryl, if you want my honest opinion.'

There could be no escaping it.

'But you must have seen something over the years of her comings and goings?'

'Hadn't much option, being as the bloody bus stop's at my garden gate. Not that there was much to see. She was off to Cambridge five mornings a week. Off to the station twice a month. Thursday used to be her day for the station bus—her day off from the shop. But these last two or three months it was Sunday. Reckon she'd other fish to fry on Thursday afternoons. She'd be out on that bike at half-past one rain or shine, regular as clockwork.'

'Shopping?'

'Not a sign of it. She did that on Wednesday evenings after work. I'd see her coming home laden.'

'Visitors?'

Shirley shook her head. 'You could count them on the fingers of one hand. The doctor, the milkman, the meter reader and her sister. Not that poor Freda was asked over very often, as far as I could see.'

'And Mr Henderson,' Dave put in.

'Oh yes, the schoolteacher. Acting Head, he is now. Picked up Martin from the house and drove him to school when he'd got this phobia thing. White as a sheet he was, poor kid. Mr Henderson is very patient—I'll say that for him. He called to collect the boy for a solid month when he first started at Browne, and another couple of weeks at the beginning of this term.'

'But he hasn't called since?'

'Not that I've noticed.' Shirley's face resumed its caution. 'But then, I'm no nosey-parker. Don't expect he got much encouragement. Cheryl didn't like the fuss about Martin's problem. Nearly ate my head off any time I mentioned it.'

'And as far as you know, Mrs Hobbs didn't have much of a social life,' Armstrong recapped. How ridiculously young he looked, with the morning sun brightening his dirty-fair hair. And he'd the kind of face that would go on looking young for decades to come, his senior reflected, mindful of the furrows in his own cheeks.

'As far as I know,' Shirley Wright was saying. 'You've put it in a nutshell, Inspector. But this is Holtchester, remember. I only get over to Cambridge once in a blue moon and I'm never in London. You needn't tell me there were no men in Cheryl Hobbs's life for I wouldn't believe you. Not after what she got up to at the Foxwillow Arms. Took her chances, same as the rest of us. But she was a pretty girl and there were more of them. *And* she enjoyed herself. Women like that don't cool down as they get older, do they, Inspector?'

Her black eyes bored into Armstrong's as she fiddled with the gunmetal pendant that defined the channel between her heavy breasts. Baxter let his colleague suffer for several long seconds before he rose to terminate the interview. As he followed their hostess down the hall past the mementoes of a dozen Mediterranean package tours, he tried but failed to select a name to fit the scent that mingled with her body odours. Joy it was not.

As they walked across the street he took grateful gulps of the cold East wind. It cleared the stink from his nostrils but not the cobwebs from his mind. The central heating lapped them as they entered Cheryl Hobbs's house, using a key from the bunch they had found in a pocket of her jeans. Baxter wandered silently about the lounge, more oppressed than usual by a sense of unwarranted intrusion upon the dead.

'What do you make of the Victoriana?' he asked Armstrong in a brusquer tone than he had intended. The Inspector ran an eye over the landscape painting, the workbox and the tea-table.

'More your line than mine. There's a lot of it around, isn't there? Maureen made me buy her one of those stripped pine dressers last month. Great brute of a thing, but the price wasn't too steep. Less than a couple of hundred.'

'You'd pay as much for that,' Baxter told him, stroking the surface of the tea-table. 'The little pieces will cost you, if they're as well made as this one. Nice piece of mahogany, too.'

'Could have been in the family.'

'Could have. Let's go upstairs. Women's bedrooms usually give one or two of their secrets away.'

The wardrobe held nothing but a modest collection of hangers carrying dresses, skirts and trousers with chain store labels. The styles were classic, the fabrics mostly plain. The choice of a woman of limited means who bought clothes to last. A woman who was conventional in her tastes or in the image she preferred to display.

The neatly folded sweaters, underwear and bedlinen that were stored in the chest-of-drawers told the same story. The folded sheets, like those on the bed, were stainfree. Contraceptives were conspicuous by their absence from bedroom and bathroom. Cheryl Hobbs's sexual activities, whatever they were, could hardly have taken place on the premises.

'Now that's worth a good, hard look.' Baxter tapped a sandalwood escritoire that had evidently doubled as a dressing-table. He squatted to squint at the elegantly tapered legs. 'Regency. None of your Edwardian repro.'

'Cost her a bob or two?'

'Don't know about *her*. But it could have set someone back fifteen hundred.'

'You don't say. Maybe she's kept the love-letters.' Armstrong tried several keys from the bunch on the lock of the single drawer, and finally opened it. Inside he found a rentbook, a bank statement and a compliment slip bearing the address and telephone number of Messrs Drew, Waters and Robinson, a Holtchester firm of solicitors. 'No clutter,' he observed in grudging admiration. 'You don't find many women without the squirrel instinct.'

'Or many men.' Baxter thought of the curious collection of discarded cutlery and plastic containers on a shelf of his colleague's garden shed. He ran a casual eye down the first page of the bank statement, and reread it with quickening pulse, before turning over. The pattern held. The record of

deposits showed not merely Cheryl's modest weekly pay
cheques but also less regular cash payments totalling between £800 and £1000 per month. Outgoings included direct
debit payments to the Housing Department, British Tele-
com and the Electricity Board and small cheques. But a
couple of months ago she had paid someone a cheque for
£5000.

Leaving Armstrong to read, mark and inwardly digest
these transactions, Baxter resumed his examination of the
escritoire.There was a sticky mark inside the front of the
drawer which indicated the removal of one label, but when
he took the drawer right out, he exposed a second in the
casing.

'"Peregrine Winterson Antiques,"' he read. '"Vesper
Terrace, off Church Street, Kensington, London W8."'

'Know the place?'

'Only from the outside. French stuff mostly. Not my cup
of tea. But the Arabs love it. Winterson must be doing well.
Should be worth a visit.'

'Think he's the London boyfriend?'

'Distinct possibility, if he's handing out this sort of stuff
as prezzies. Why don't you nip up to Town this afternoon
and find out?'

Armstrong's spirits sank. City lights held few attractions
for him, especially on fine Saturday afternoons when Holtchester United were playing at home.

Martin's bedroom with its small collections of clothes,
books and sketches didn't detain them for long. Nor did
the clinical bathroom. But just inside the back door their
attention was caught by a pair of mud-streaked wellington
boots.

'She could have been gardening,' Baxter observed. The
window above the kitchen sink overlooked a tidy but feature-
less lawn and border.

'Suppose so.' Applying minimal pressure from hand-
kerchief-wrapped fingers, Armstrong upturned each boot in

turn. Mud wedged the spaces between heel and sole, and an orange beech leaf lay entrapped in one of these deposits. 'For what it's worth,' he remarked with that occasional mock-diffidence that drove his senior to distraction, 'I find it hard to credit a fellow called Peregrine Winterson with a passion for the big outdoors.'

'No,' Baxter agreed, leading the way back to the car. 'But there are beeches on the banks of the Cam. And *pieds-à-terre* with a view of the river. Sort of thing that might very well have appealed to him.' And before the day was over, Armstrong should be in a position to confirm or deny his hypothesis.

Back at the station the Chief Inspector returned the call that had been made in his absence by the Director of Social Services.

'This care and protection order for the Hobbs child . . .'

'I thought you had everything tied up. Magistrate seemed to accept the need for a place of safety . . . you told me you'd wangled a place in that Norfolk home—Whitefields, is it?'

'Whitelands. Yes, we were lucky there. It's a well-run place, low absconding rate. Very suitable for a temporary placement. Problem is, the aunt's been on to us. Wants to know where we're sending him, so that she can keep in touch by letter and telephone. Warden would retain discretion over visits, of course. She seems a stable type, and the kid needs some sort of family support, God knows. So we'd like to give her the information. But in view of the physical danger . . .'

Baxter thought quickly. If Freda Taylor was told of Martin's whereabouts, she would almost certainly share that knowledge with Stephen Hobbs. 'As far as I'm concerned you can go ahead,' he said. 'The boy's in no danger from his father or his aunt.'

Before he had finished speaking the words he began to

doubt them. But he put down the receiver all the same, and forced himself to concentrate on the tasks that lay ahead.

CHAPTER 8

'I'd put the estate at fifteen thousand,' said Herbert Waters, scrutinizing the bundle of share certificates purchased on Cheryl Hobbs's behalf by a London firm of brokers over the last three years. 'Nothing spectacular.' He smiled at the detectives from behind his grandfather's mahogany desk.

'Not bad for a single mother on eighty pounds a week. Don't suppose the alimony amounted to much,' Baxter observed.

'No, looking at it like that. Not bad. I dare say she had good friends . . . a pretty girl like that. Not that I would wish to give the wrong impression. I'm sure she paid her taxes.'

From the wall behind his grandson, Herbert Waters the First stared imperiously at the horizon. Not a man to smile easily, Baxter guessed.

'And the will?'

'Perfectly straightforward. Everything goes to the boy except for a thousand to her sister who is named as executor.'

Freda Taylor might have killed for other motives, but not, surely, for a thousand pounds.

'Anything else you can tell us?'

'No . . . I don't think so. Except perhaps that Mrs Hobbs told me two or three months ago that she was contemplating house purchase.'

'Buying her council house?'

Waters shook his head. 'That was what I advised. It would have paid her. But no. She couldn't wait to be out of the estate. And she'd set her sights much higher. Wanted a detached place with a bit of land.'

'For fifteen thousand?'

'No, no. Mrs Hobbs wasn't naïve. She was contemplating joint ownership. Her idea was to put down a substantial deposit. For the first few years of the marriage her future husband would take major responsibility for mortgage repayments.'

'And later?'

'She had plans to set up in business on her own account, and in a few years time she expected to have a substantial income.'

'What sort of business?'

'She was evasive.'

'And the husband? Did she tell you anything about him?'

'Nothing.'

'Was she in love, do you think?'

Waters looked embarrassed. The old man in the portrait would not have been so easily discomfited, Baxter told himself. Neither would he have taken on the likes of Cheryl Hobbs as a client.

'In love? I don't suppose so.' Waters smirked. 'But I'm not in the habit of speculating on these things.'

'Little bitch,' Armstrong muttered as they walked out of the building.

'Oh yes?'

'She was just using him, this man she was going to marry. As a stepping-stone to the sweet life.'

'Perhaps—as she had been used.'

'Who by?'

'Daddy, for one. Oh, I dare say there may not have been physical abuse. But it sounds as though he exploited her emotionally.' And how many others? They might have to dig a lot of dirt to expose the crucial relationship. As they set off for lunch at the station he thought enviously of Sarah's diminished pile of garden rubbish.

*

Hilde Tomlinson was wearing a faded mustard sweater and tweed skirt as she showed them into a back room that caught the early afternoon sun. It was attractively furnished. A tall vase of michaelmas daisies stood in the Edwardian fireplace. Sanded boards gleamed mellowly underfoot. The two abstract paintings had all the precision of the pattern on the oriental rug.

'You were lucky to catch me,' Hilde told the detectives. 'I was just going out to help Phyllis, and we don't always hear the bell from the garden.'

Baxter looked through the French windows at the bent figure working on the herbaceous border. It was an interesting garden, and earlier in the year it must have been very attractive. He liked the curving path, the espaliers, the contrast between highly groomed and wild patches.

'Very nice. You designed it yourself?'

'Phyllis—my friend—did most of it. I lack visual imagination. And she does most of the donkey work too, I'm afraid. More time on her hands. But I don't suppose this is a social call, Chief Inspector. Any news?'

'Not yet,' he answered gravely. 'But I've a few more questions.'

'Oh.' She waved them towards two easy chairs and sat down on a carver. 'Fire ahead.'

'I should like to ask you about the gap in your casenotes.'

'Gap?' Baxter got the impression that she was willing her body to conceal her anxiety.

'Last February. You began an entry and abandoned it.'

'What gives you that idea?'

'The impression on the next page.'

Her colour rose in spite of herself. 'Well?'

'Why did you do it, Mrs Tomlinson?'

'I am not answerable to you for my clinical practices.'

'Except when they are relevant to my inquiry. Cheryl Hobbs said something that day which unnerved you, something which overthrew the habits of your life-work. What was it?'

The colour had drained from her face now. She was staring over their heads into a mirror on the wall behind them.

'Nothing relevant to her murder.'

'How can you be so sure—considering that a third party was involved? Shall I remind you of what you wrote?'

Her dark eyes met his. 'No need. I remember very well. Mrs Hobbs made some assertions about my relationship with my friend Phyllis—Mrs Steele. Said we were Lesbians —but her term was derogatory.'

'And that threw you—a trained and experienced social worker? Surely you must have been at the receiving end of a good deal of personal abuse?'

'Of myself, yes. But not of my friends. I've always tried to keep my private life private.'

'Ah, yes. We had wondered, you see, if the "P" in your notes might stand for Peter Denny, as it did in some of the other entries.'

'No!' She was entirely herself again, and he knew that they would never shift her. Not under the Judges' rules. She was smiling, damn her.

'Of course I should have completed that entry, Chief Inspector. What stopped me wasn't prudishness or concern for my friend's reputation but professional pride. I'd over-reacted to Cheryl's taunts. Stepped out of the caseworker role. The result was a therapeutically useless session which I was ashamed to record.'

'Dr Denny didn't object?'

'Heavens, no. I explained what had happened and he accepted it without a murmur. He's far less obsessional than I am about casenotes.'

Baxter rose abruptly. 'A good try, Mrs Tomlinson, but not good enough.'

'Really, Chief Inspector.' She hadn't expected that, this

woman who evidently went for gold in everything she attempted. Lying included.

'Got nowhere fast, that time,' Armstrong observed, as the front door closed behind them.

'Oh, I don't know,' Baxter spoke with a show of optimism. '*She* won't crack but Denny might when he gets the wind up. Especially if his wife is giving him a rough weekend.'

They drove back to the station in silence, Baxter anticipating another pleasurable spell of solitary cogitation, and Armstrong worrying about his impending trip to London. He had never learnt the knack of chatting up arty types with names like Peregrine Winterson, and he never would. Maybe, just maybe, the computer trace they'd requested before lunch would give him a lead-in.

'Bloody hell.' He stood in the communications room, contemplating the two-line message with disbelief.

'What's this supposed to mean?' he asked Baxter in the privacy of his office. The Chief Inspector read the printout: ' "Illegal request. Information on this individual available to senior officers only on a need-to-know basis." One for the old man, I'm afraid.' He relocated his peppermint in the corner of his mouth and rang the Chief Constable.

Five minutes later he had a reply. Armstrong watched his face cloud over.

'For some reason or other, this fellow's to have the kid glove treatment. Chief insists that I go up to Town and interview him myself with someone from the Met to see fair play.'

'For Christ's sake. So what would you like me to do?'

'Go over all the evidence with a toothcomb. Keep an eye on the bods in the incidents room. They could do with some morale boosting, I imagine.'

'Tea?' Superintendent Caskey's fastidious Plantagenet face clashed with the Lowry prints and potted cacti which some-

one had imported into the office in New Scotland Yard.
Baxter guessed that his regular workplace was elsewhere.
Caskey examined the contents of the pot with close attention and surveyed the results of his judicious stir with a
satisfaction that suggested he might have felt as much at
home in the production as in the control side of the drugs
trade.

'Tedious business for you, Chief Inspector,' he murmured, handing Baxter a cup and saucer. 'Sorry we had to
drag you up here.'

'But Mr Winterson has special status, I gather? And we
don't grass on our grasses.'

'Not in hard copy, anyhow.'

'You'll appreciate that I need to know, Superintendent.'

'Mmhm. Let me fill you in.' Caskey laid down his tea-
spoon. 'We gave Winterson his new identity for services
rendered. A mite high profile for our taste, but it was what
he wanted. Look at these before-and-after shots. You'd
never tell, would you?'

Baxter studied the photographs in the plastic folder. A
mousey young man had become a blonde middle-aged one.
The face under the expensive-looking wig was strangely
austere.

'Alopecia helped a lot. Eyebrows all gone, you see. He's
bald as a coot now.'

'Poor bastard.'

'Don't waste any pity on Peregrine. He's doing very
nicely.'

'And the services rendered?'

'Spiked an East Anglian heroin network in '74. Walter
Craig he was then—Deputy Manager of a Holtchester hotel
called the Foxwillow Arms. Know it?'

'Before my time with Mid-Anglia. But I've heard of it.'

'Shabby, easygoing outfit by all accounts. But it did well
enough from local and commercial trade. Pulled in some
tourists too in the summer. Then the pushers got their foot

in the door. Place became a major communications centre. Manager was paid a packet to keep his mouth shut. Craig was kept in the dark—or so he says. Cheesed off, he was. He'd taken the job for good management experience, and he wasn't getting it. Boss was losing interest in his regular trade. Then the old man became careless about his second string—depressed, maybe. Craig got on to the truth without really trying.'

'And he squealed?'

'Not for two or three months. Not until he'd accumulated an information package worth selling.'

'And he did a deal with you? A one-off?'

'Not exactly.' Caskey crumbled a Petit Beurre. 'We have what you might call an open-ended relationship. Mr Winterson is blessed with a photographic memory. Considerable asset in the antiques trade, I should imagine. We don't ask too much, but every now and then he helps us with an identification. No names, no pack drill, no court appearances.'

'So you want me to tread gently?'

'If you please. With the recent resurgence of heroin Winterson is more valuable than ever.'

'But murder is murder.'

'Unfortunately.' Caskey's nose wrinkled as though he would have liked to refute the assertion. 'If you should deem it necessary to resort to more stringent procedures, I must ask you to advise me before acting.'

'But . . .'

'Sorry, Chief Inspector. The issue is not negotiable. Your Chief Constable understands the situation. One other thing. Mr Winterson's *alter ego* is not for publication to your Holtchester colleagues. Or to Inspector Plumb, who'll be making the trip with you. He's waiting in the foyer.'

'Mind the tube?' The chubby London detective wore the three-piece, pink shirt and toothbrush moustache of the archetypal Young Fogey. 'Parking can be hairy in South Ken.'

'That doesn't bother me, but what about my clothes?' Baxter surveyed his well-cut but unfashionable tweed overcoat. 'We don't look as though we belonged.'

'With a bit of luck nobody except Winterson will be around to notice. That type of business is usually shut on Saturday afternoons. But if not, you could always be my uncle. Up from the country on a shopping spree.'

'Charming.' Baxter pulled down his hatbrim and set his companion a sharpish pace in the teeth of a rising gale.

The middle-aged woman who greeted them first on the intercom and then at the door of the empty shop accepted the story without demur. The sky was darkening now, but Baxter was glad their guide made no move to switch on the lights as she led them across the ground floor to the lift. The funereal marble and elaborate gilding of French Empire furniture were not to his taste. And as the lift doors opened on Peregrine Winterson's private rooms, he discovered that they were not to his host's taste either. The dwarf bookcases and low tables lacked fussy detail which could so easily have distracted from the elegance of their Regency design. The other furniture and furnishings—two settees in blonde leather, cream rugs and carpets, and a pair of standard lamps—were unaggressively modern. The tall figure who rose to greet them wore a caramel coloured cardigan and tan trousers which blended pleasingly with the colours of his habitat.

As soon as the woman, whom he introduced as his secretary-receptionist, had retired to her office, Winterson drew the curtains and switched on the lights.

'Drinks?' he asked, helping himself to a brandy. 'Don't worry, it's only my second. I knew you'd be coming as soon as I read about Cheryl in the paper. You or someone like you. And I knew I'd get no peace unless I saw you. Sorry.'

'That's all right,' Plumb assured him. 'We don't often see welcome written on the mat.'

Going to be a nuisance, was he? 'I'm the one with the questions,' Baxter interposed with as much flippancy as he could muster. 'Inspector Plumb is here to make sure I ask them politely.'

'I see.' Winterson raised his glass in mock courtesy. 'Welcome, gentlemen. Nice to be taken care of.'

'As you took care of Cheryl Hobbs?'

'If only she'd let me. I wanted to, you know. Right from the start.'

'At the Foxwillow Arms?'

'They told you about that? Yes, of course, they'd have to. Offered her marriage then, God help me. Always knew I was going places—Cheryl did too. She wanted me to strike out on my own, buy a business.'

'Like Daddy?'

'I suppose so. But I wasn't ready and she wasn't prepared to wait. Under-manager's money wasn't any good to her.'

'So she settled for Steve Hobbs?'

'Against my advice. Her idea was to have her cake and eat it. But Steve was the conventional type. Wanted her all to himself.'

'And the marriage broke up. You left Holtchester. But you kept in touch?'

'Till the end.' His voice broke. 'Sorry. It's bloody hard to realize it *is* the end. Oh, I had other women—men too. But Cheryl was different. Cheryl was the light of my life. Crazy, isn't it?' He drained his glass.

Baxter paused for a couple of seconds before continuing: 'When did you last see her, Mr Winterson?'

'Last Sunday.'

'Sunday, not Thursday. You're sure?'

'Positive. The wound's still raw. Thursday used to be one of our days together. I took her round the salerooms. But not recently.' He consulted a pocket diary. 'Not since the third week of June.'

'Then how did you spend last Thursday afternoon?'

Winterson shrugged. 'Couple of hours in the salerooms, couple of hours at the health club. Squash, massage, jacuzzi. Great place for erotic fantasies, the jacuzzi.'

'You could provide witnesses?'

'If necessary. But I do hope it won't prove necessary.'

'Probably not. All the same, I'd be glad if you could write down the names and places while they're fresh in your memory. Seal up the list in an envelope if you like, and we'll give it to Superintendent Caskey for safekeeping. You're acquainted, I understand?'

'In a manner of speaking. Very well, if I must. My writing things are next door.'

He returned a few minutes later with a handwritten list which he displayed to the detectives at a prudent distance before inserting it in an envelope. Baxter accepted the offering and immediately handed it over to Plumb, who was looking uneasy.

'I understand Mrs Hobbs had plans to remarry,' Baxter prompted.

'But she didn't propose to marry me, if I may anticipate your next question. We'd come to know ourselves better over the years. We both needed our escape hatches. Marriage would have spoilt everything between us.'

'Who was he then?'

'I've no idea. She didn't volunteer the information, and I was too proud to ask. One of her dons, I expect.'

'She had a collection?'

'They were her bread and butter.'

'And you didn't care?'

'Of course I cared. But I'd no right. I'd sold her the theory of love-making as an art at the Foxwillow Arms, and she'd proved herself an artist. Told myself she was being appreciated. Oh, I know there are some crude customers in the groves of Academe these days. But I imagine they're a shade more discriminating than the types she slept with in the old days.'

'Where did she meet the academics?'

Winterson shook his head. 'Didn't ask. In pubs, I expect.'

'Or in the bookshop?'

'Perhaps. She was cagey with me.'

'And you with her? How deep was she into the drugs racket?'

'Not at all. Didn't hear anything either—from me. Wouldn't be where I am today if I hadn't learnt to keep my mouth shut.'

'But there must have been some bigmouths in and out of the Foxwillow Arms. You must have talked about the old days now and then.'

'Never. We had other interests. I'd like to show you something.'

The detectives followed him out of his apartment and up a flight of stairs to a huge workroom.

Baxter wrinkled his nose. 'The Empire in decay.'

'Plenty of latter-day Napoleons would take a different view,' Winterson reminded him. And there was evidence of heavy investment in the work of restoration. They walked on sawdust and inhaled the mingled odours of dust, dryrot, preservative and lacquer. Damaged and deteriorated furniture stood around in various stages of rehabilitation. Their guide unlocked a door in a partition wall.

No dirt or disorder here. Just row upon row of chairs.

'Good God.'

'Hundred and forty-eight. All in mint condition. And every one Cheryl's. They were to be her stock-in-trade. I was storing them till she had her own premises.'

'Your wedding presents?'

'Two or three. But she bought the bulk of them from the salerooms. With her cash in my name. She had this marvellous knack for wheeling and dealing. I helped her get her eye in, but the instinct was there.'

'Why chairs?'

'They display well and there's always a market. And obviously they're more portable than the heavy stuff. Cheryl had this thing about feeling in physical control of her possessions.'

Baxter walked between the rows of chairs for several minutes, fingering the carving, inspecting the undersides of seats. The pieces were indeed in good condition. Repairs had been competent and discreet. Dates ranged from the eighteenth to the mid twentieth centuries. He did mental sums for the sample he could identify.

'How much is it worth?'

Winterson shrugged. 'Market can be jumpy. Somewhere between ten and fifteen grand.'

The Chief Inspector had no reason to suppose he was underestimating.

'You needn't have shown us.'

'Nothing in it for me, you mean? Sorry if I'm spoiling your stereotypes. But there's the boy to think of.'

'Did you see much of him?'

Winterson shook his head. 'Not since he was a toddler. No point really. It would have been too risky. Besides . . . I'm no good with kids.'

'You'll get in touch with Mrs Hobbs's solicitors? Drew, Waters and . . .' he fished for their card.

'Robinson. I've already drafted the letter. Put her on to them myself, you know. D, W and R were *the* establishment firm in my Holtchester days. Just the right chaps for a girl who was getting off the game.'

'One-all. Pretty miserable performance.' Plumb was reading the Arsenal–Chelsea score from a television screen in a shop window.

'Oh, I don't know,' Baxter growled, plunging his gloved

hands deep in his pockets. He had toyed with the idea of picking up Louie's critique of the Poulencs' price list while he was in town, and decided against it. Saturday evening encounters with ex-colleagues were rarely brief. And the provincial uncle in him was eager to head for home.

At a quarter to seven he walked with a brisk step into the incidents room where Detective-Sergeant Short and a clerk-typist were alone on duty.

'How goes it?'

'Chugging away, sir. Checking up alibis, mostly.' Short had learnt the hard way that the Chief Inspector disliked being overburdened with insignificant detail.

'Anything else?'

'There's this, sir. Constable Browning spotted it in the *News*. Inspector Armstrong thought you might be interested.'

Baxter read the cutting. '"Bedsitter to let central Cambridge. Suit quiet business person or student." I take it you've traced the number?'

'We already knew it. Belongs to J. C. Poulenc of Pepper Street.'

CHAPTER 9

A light went out in the village street. Baxter's habitual waking-signal. His lids fluttered open and he consulted his watch. Seven-five. The days were shrinking fast. In a couple of weeks they'd be out of official summertime.

Summertime, for Christ's sake. From the bathroom window he saw gulls circling over the ploughed fields. He returned to the bedroom and sat down on the bed. Sarah's waking-signal. She reached up sleepily for his wrist.

'Sunday?'

'Mm-hm.'

'Coming back to bed?'

'For a while. I haven't long, pet.'

'Long enough.'

He climbed back under the duvet, nervous as a schoolboy before the weekly ritual they had learnt the hard way not to take for granted. It was one of their good days. After a slow start, things went right. Beautifully and variously right.

Armstrong was waiting at the station with a request for Baxter to ring back the Chief Constable.

'How goes it?' Montgomery barked.

'So-so. You've seen my interim report?'

'I'd like a chat. This London visit . . . Met's a bit scratchy.'

'Yes, sir. I'm pushed this morning, I'm afraid . . .'

'Look in before lunch, then. You'll find me at home.'

Like nine Sundays out of ten, Baxter thought. Francis Montgomery had all the self-protective instincts of the Norman barons from whom he was descended.

'London trip any use?' Armstrong asked.

'Not a lot. Winterson said he wouldn't have been Cheryl Hobbs's second spouse. And I rather think he was telling the truth. She was planning to set up in the antique furniture trade and he was storing stock for her. A business association.'

'Nothing else?'

'That's all I'm allowed to say.'

'I see. Where do we go from here?'

'To the Poulencs. According to a couple of Charing Cross Road sources they were overcharging. We need to know how they make a living from selling pricey books to people who should know better.'

'And renting out rooms, perhaps?'

'Ah, yes. Now that was interesting, very interesting. Remind me to pat Browning on the back. Suppose I'd better see what the lads have dug up on the Poulencs.' Armstrong passed the relevant briefing across his senior's desk. 'Mmm. Whiter than white, by the look of this. Both from well-known Normandy families. Active in the Resistance—suppose that's when they became Anglophiles. Married during the war and moved to Cambridge soon afterwards. Old boy seems to have been active on the cultural scene—Festival Committee, Friends of the Fitzwilliam. Must have dithered a bit about citizenship—they were naturalized in '64. Had a shop in King's Parade until '77. Sold up for health reasons —apparently Jean-Claude's got one of those slow, progressive diseases of the central nervous system. Can't get my tongue round it. Had to give up most of his valuation work, it seems: he's something of an expert in old bindings. Son helped in the business for a few years, but his wife was a Parisian and she couldn't adapt.'

'To Cambridge or to mother-in-law?'

Baxter laughed. 'It doesn't say. Marie didn't have any sort of public life, as far as I can see. But they must have entertained quite a lot when the going was good. I'd guess she kept a good table.'

'So the move to Pepper Street would have been traumatic for her. Loss of status, security . . .'

'But she hasn't lost her husband—yet. I suspect she'd give up a lot to support him.'

They drove the ten miles to Cambridge through light Sunday traffic. There was already a sprinkling of tourists and pious undergrads on Magdalene Street, but the bleaker environs of East Road were bereft of pedestrians. In Pepper Street there was nobody to be seen except an elderly woman with a dog on a lead and a Sunday paper tucked under her arm. The window of the bookshop, like those of the other business premises, was shuttered and padlocked.

Marie Poulenc answered the door promptly, her face icing over in recognition.

'May we come in, Madame?'

'Certainly. I don't conduct my business on the doorstep.'
She looked to right and left. The woman with the dog had
disappeared.

Several dozen books were stacked on the table in the back
room, and one lay open in the old man's lap. He sat slumped
in his chair. Impossible to tell whether he was reading or
sleeping or listening to the music programme playing loudly
on the portable radio. His eyes opened and his body jerked
as his wife switched off the set.

'Some refreshments, gentlemen? It's too early for sherry,
I imagine. Coffee, perhaps?' Marie Poulenc indicated a
couple of spindly chairs.

Baxter shook his head. 'I see you are letting a room,
Madame.'

'We are naturalized British citizens, Chief Inspector,'
Jean-Claude objected. 'We prefer the English usage.'

Baxter grunted an apology.

'Yes, we have advertised,' the old man continued, 'and
the room has been taken. A perfectly legal transaction.'

'We're not questioning its legality but . . .'

'Won't you please sit down?' Marie repeated. 'Looking
up imposes an intolerable strain on my husband.'

'Certainly.' The detectives lowered themselves cautiously
on to tapestry-covered seats.

'What we are requesting, Mr Poulenc, is your permission
to search the vacant room—if it is still unoccupied.'

'There is a saying, isn't there, that an Englishman's home
in his castle.' The old freedom fighter had few freedoms left,
Baxter thought.

'Indeed. But you have indicated that this apartment in
your castle is surplus to your personal requirements. May
I ask whether it was previously used for business or domestic
purposes?'

'If you can give me a good reason for answering.'

'Certainly. Our inquiries suggest that Mrs Hobbs had a
number of friends in Cambridge. Including men friends.'

'Hardly surprising,' Marie Poulenc retorted. 'She was a very attractive young woman.'

'And of recent years she went out rather seldom in the evenings.'

'Well?'

'It is therefore possible that she met some of these friends in working hours. And on your premises.'

'Possible but not probable,' Jean-Claude objected. 'This is a bookshop, not a social club.'

'I am employed to explore possibilities, Mr Poulenc. One of these friends may have been Cheryl Hobbs's murderer. I should therefore be glad to know the purpose to which you put this room and your reason for letting it.'

'It is quite simple, Chief Inspector.' Marie spoke with quiet authority. 'It was originally a bedroom. When my husband could no longer manage the stairs—three or four years ago—we began to sleep in the room behind this.' She waved a hand towards one of two doors.

'That was about the time Cheryl Hobbs came to work for you?'

'Shortly afterwards.'

'You might have used the spare room for surplus stock. But you didn't?'

'No, we left it as it was. We had accumulated a considerable number of books that didn't deserve shelf space. With Cheryl's help, we made a grand clearance. We liked the idea of having a second bedroom. My son and daughter-in-law used it from time to time. And I sewed there.'

'Did Cheryl Hobbs ever use it?'

'Never,' Jean-Claude asserted.

'Occasionally.' Marie's hand reached for the invalid's shoulder. 'My husband's memory is not what it was. Cheryl slept there occasionally if she came back on a late train from London.'

'Alone.'

'Naturally.' Her voice was steady but he read fear in her eyes.

Baxter stood up. 'I should like to search the room now. With your permission.'

She rose. 'You may go as you please. The spare bedroom is on the second floor.'

Baxter turned to the man in the wheelchair. Poulenc twisted his fine head upwards and sideways.

'Do what you wish. It won't bring her back, will it?'

The stairs were steep and uncarpeted. There was a faint smell of damp rot. Several of the steel engravings hung on the left-hand wall were spoilt by foxing. They paused briefly on the first floor landing to glance into two rooms lined with bookshelves. Two doors led off the second floor landing— one to a bathroom, and the second, which had been fitted with a Yale lock but now lay open, to a bedroom. Baxter opened the door of the mirror-fronted wardrobe and sniffed.

'Come on, Bill. Your nose is younger than mine. What do you get?' He drew back and Armstrong stuck in his head.

'Lavender—furniture polish, I suppose. And mothballs. Didn't think they still made the things.'

'Anything else? Try the far corners.'

His companion bent over awkwardly, avoiding physical contact with the wood.

'Well?'

'It's. the girl's scent all right. The stuff she had on her when she copped it. What did Mason say it was called?'

'Joy.' Baxter made a business of unpacking the aspirators and plastic bags from his investigation case. 'Will you take the dressing-table?' He switched on one of the battery-operated instruments and sucked dust from the bottom corners of the wardrobe interior. Holding the plastic bag to the light, he saw something glinting. A sequin.

'How are you doing?' he asked.

'Nothing obvious.' Armstrong held up a bag of greyish dust.

'We'll try the space behind the drawers. Here—it's a four-handed job.' With gloved hands they eased out the newly lined drawer of the wardrobe. More grey dust and a lipsticked tissue. Then the drawers of the dressing-table. Behind the lowest they found a crumpled piece of flame-coloured satin. Baxter shook it out.

'What shall I write on the label?'

'Camiknicks, you fool. Doesn't Maureen . . .?'

'None of your business. The mattress?'

'Bit obvious, I reckon.' It was dustfree on both sides. 'Let's go down.'

Marie Poulenc awaited them at the foot of the stairs, her hands clasped in front of her black skirt. 'Do you wish to search our bedroom?'

'I should be more interested in your dustbin.' Baxter was within a foot of her when he said it. Close enough to hear her sharp intake of breath. Then she turned on her heel and led the two men down the passage and through a dark kitchen to an enclosed yard. She watched silently, arms folded across her stomach, as they unwrapped the newspaper packages of refuse and picked out the scraps of cut-up lingerie in flame, turquoise and black.

'I wanted to burn them,' she said when they had finished. 'But my husband would have noticed. We never burn rubbish. Jean-Claude has a horror of fire, of being trapped. His best friend was incinerated in a locomotive shed in '42. He had to hide near the fuse boxes when the guards came.' She shivered. 'You don't forget such things.'

'He didn't know about Cheryl's activities? Are you sure?' Baxter guided her back into the kitchen and sat her on a wooden chair.

She shook her head, tears running down her face. 'It was easy to deceive him. Some of our customers browse for hours on end. It's a matter of pride that we don't disturb them.

Besides, Jean-Claude's hearing is poor and he sleeps a good deal.' She wiped her eyes with a small, lace-edged handkerchief.

'I did it for him, you know. Entirely for him. I should not like you to think we were profiteers.' A word with a painful history. 'Cheryl gave me back £10 from her pay—almost nothing. It paid for a few groceries.'

'But she brought in the customers. How many?'

'Twenty or thirty regulars, I suppose. Yes, without them we couldn't have kept the business going. It means every-thing to Jean-Claude. His *raison-d'être*.'

'Marie! *Qu'est ce que tu fais?*' the sick man called, his consonants slurring.

'*Je viens*. Don't tell him, will you. Not yet.'

'Sooner or later . . . There may well be a prosecution.'

'I know. But it will be easier if I break it to him. When we're alone. The disease makes it difficult for him to control his emotions. The shame . . .'

They returned to the tiny living-room.

Jean-Claude looked up with a smile. He seemed more relaxed now. His wasted right hand held open the book on his lap, not at a page of text but at the whorled design inside the cover. His eye caught Baxter's quick admiring glance.

'Lovely, isn't it? The work of a compatriot. Are you interested in bookbinding, Chief Inspector?'

'Sadly ignorant.'

'Each to his last. I was discourteous earlier on. Please excuse me. My temper is not what it was. If you have found anything that brings you nearer the murderer . . .'

'Not really. I shall need your help there. I should like a list of your customers over the past year. Particularly your regular customers.'

The old man frowned. 'That won't be easy. In the old days I knew them nearly all by name. But these young people come and go . . . Cash transactions, mostly.'

'But you'll try? With Mrs Poulenc's help? We'll call back tomorrow.'

'You certainly gave them an easy ride,' Armstrong grumbled as they belted up for the return journey. 'Dirty business— letting for immoral purposes. Do you believe she kept it from the old man?'

'Yes. Don't you?'

'I suppose so. She'd have had practice in lying if the Maquis was all it's cracked up to be. Wonder if they'll tell the truth about their clientèle.'

'We know the front runner, don't we?'

'Gordon?'

'Mm. French scholar. Wife working at the clinic. Unbeatable combination, isn't it?'

'If you say so,' Armstrong conceded in a tone that suggested yearnings for stones unturned and avenues unexplored.

After a brief onslaught on an accumulating pile of administrative chores at headquarters, he drove to the Chief Constable's home near Newmarket. It was an ugly interwar villa in stockbroker Tudor. Montgomery ushered him into his study, which overlooked the rockery.

'Fine show today, sir,' Baxter observed in the manner which was expected of him. To his eyes the disposition of plants and rocks was horribly contrived and un-English.

'Not a heath man, are you?' Montgomery dispensed the Croft Original.

'Not any sort of horticulturalist. But I like the smell of the soil.'

'Ah, but there's soil *and* soil, isn't there? Alpines are fussier than you'd give them credit for. Takes a bit of experience to get the right balance.'

'And you've succeeded.'

'So it would seem, Dick. So it would seem. Now about this murder . . .'

'Yes, sir?'

'Met have been griping. Say you gave Winterson a rough-ish ride.'

'Has he complained?'

'Not that I know of. I gather the assessment was based on Inspector Plumb's report.'

'Hardly best evidence, sir. I doubt if Plumb has much experience of murder investigations.'

'Or you of the current drug scene?'

'*Touché*. But with luck I've finished with Winterson. Just as well. His alibi implicated half the clientèle of Sotheby's.'

'Jesus Christ.' Montgomery drained his sherry glass. 'Then there's the clinic. The sooner you get the staff off the hook the sooner we can restore public confidence.'

'Point taken.' As Baxter tensed up, his stomach acids engaged in unholy alliance with the invading sherry. 'I'm doing my best, sir, but cooperation hasn't been a hundred per cent.'

'No?'

He reminded his host of the incomplete file entry and indicated his doubts about Hilde Tomlinson's explanation.

'Good God, man. You're hard to satisfy. Do you really expect me to believe that a woman with her reputation would invent a lie that embarrassed her closest friend?'

'Assuming it *was* a lie.'

'Oh, I'd stake my reputation on that one, Dick. I played golf for a good ten years with Arnie Tomlinson. Nice, quiet, steady bloke. Built up a good-sized tannery business, married late in life. One son. Danny's in Israel—bit of a fire-eater in his way, but Arnie was proud of him. And proud of Hilde. She's a strong woman, but she nearly went to pieces when Arnie died. Oh, there's no doubt in my mind that that was a love-match.'

'And Phyllis Steele?'

'Don't know the lady personally. Widowed young, I understand, and went back to nursing. Ran the children's ward in Holtchester Hospital for umpteen years. And very well too, my wife told me. She knew her from various charity committees. Suppose that's how Hilde met her too. They've shared a house for three or four years now—all open and above board. Matter of fact, Phyllis Steele has an admirer. Wife pointed him out to me at a Horticultural Society do. Cactus man. After her for years, apparently, in a half-hearted way. Not the type a sensible woman would get too involved with.'

'No, sir.' Baxter managed with difficulty to maintain his sobriety.

'Sooner you resolve this matter the better, Dick. Hilde Tomlinson is highly regarded in Mid-Anglia. Last thing we want is a martyr on our hands. Any other leads?'

The story of the bookshop revelations earned the Chief Inspector the offer of an unwanted second glass of sherry but nothing in the way of encouragement.

'You know what this is likely to stir up, don't you? A full-blown university scandal. We've enough town-gown aggro in Cambridge these days without one of those.'

'It shouldn't come to that.'

'It had better not.' The CC scowled as if at a candidate for a detention centre. Baxter smouldered as he drove home for lunch.

His temper was tested again three hours later when he and Armstrong visited Newnham. The marmalade cat was grooming itself on the Gordons' doorstep, submitting first one and then the other back leg to careful inspection. But there was no reply to the doorbell and no car parked nearby. As they turned to leave, they saw the curtains twitch in the house next door. As the Gordons' neighbour emerged they caught a glimpse of group photographs in his hall. He was a small neat man in his early seventies. A retired university servant perhaps, and a cat lover, to judge by its warm welcome. A man who probably told the truth to policemen.

'They're out, I'm afraid,' he volunteered, on sight of their identification. 'They've a cottage on the coast they go to most weekends. Somewhere near Southwold—haven't got the exact address.'

'Never mind. Tomorrow will do.' Baxter hoped he was right, remembering the vulnerability of the child in care. 'Are we likely to find Dr Andrew Gordon at home on a Monday morning?'

'Not in term. He works in college most mornings in term —if you can call Landers a college.'

CHAPTER 10

'How would you rate it?' Baxter asked Armstrong next morning as they stood in the car park of Landers, youngest of the Cambridge colleges.

'Bloody awful.' The Inspector's touchstones for academic architecture were renaissance Cambridge and the Victorian Tudor of Queen's University, Belfast. 'Couldn't see myself settling down to work in a place like that.'

The foundation of a confectionery giant, who was said to have taken a hand in its design, Landers stands just outside the city boundary on the Colchester Road. Local controversy raged as its flamboyant cupolas and turrets took shape, and the final product was held to have been a contributing factor to at least one traffic accident.

To all appearances, Andrew Gordon had adapted well to his baroque habitat. His small pink-washed room with its curving balcony had the look of a well-organized office. In addition to the inevitable bookcases there were two filing cabinets and several box files on the rosewood desk. There was, however, no computer terminal. The Parian busts and political posters were hardly the choice of an upwardly mobile Organization Man. And the inkstains on their owner's pink shirt might have raised an eyebrow at a sales conference.

'Sit down, gentlemen. I've been expecting you.' Gordon spoke with an Edinburgh accent less refined than his wife's. He was a man in his late thirties, with fine, dark hair and a pale oval face. Brown eyes glowed behind his glasses. Shaved of its small beard, the jaw might have looked weak.

'How can I help you?' he asked, gesturing towards four chairs with writing flaps, obviously intended for students. The two detectives selected the outer pair, manœuvring them so as to achieve the possibility of eye contact with each other as well as their informant. Gordon sat forward in the chair behind the desk, hands clasping elbows in the gesture of a tense man trying to look relaxed.

'Would you kindly take us through your activities on Thursday afternoon and evening,' Baxter asked.

Gordon sighed. 'Went to the University Library around two-thirty. Tea in the library cafeteria between four and four-twenty. Then I walked home. Walking unblocks the thinking processes—shakes up the cerebellum, they tell me. Then it was work . . . supper . . . work . . . bed. The usual pattern.'

'But Thursday was rather unusual, wasn't it?'

'I don't think I'm with you.'

'Your wife said something about a celebration.'

'Told you that, did she?' Gordon scratched his chin. 'Yes, she was a month gone. Well and truly pregnant.'

'A big occasion?'

'We'd been trying for years . . . off and on.'

'Congratulations.' He picked up a ruler. 'Any more questions?'

'Did your wife mention Cheryl Hobbs over supper on Thursday?'

'As a matter of fact, she did. Told me about the Mason

fellow inviting Mrs Hobbs to use the clinic typewriter. Rather tickled about it, Jane was. Against all the rules of human resources therapy, apparently. But when the cat's away . . .'

'Was Mrs Hobbs's name familiar to you? Had your wife mentioned her on earlier occasions?'

'Once or twice. Said she had a son in treatment. But Mrs H reckoned his school did more for him than the clinic and Jane was inclined to agree.'

'Did your wife ever meet Mrs Hobbs?'

'I believe not.' Gordon stood the ruler on its end, holding it down with the lightest possible pressure.

'Unlike you.'

'I don't quite . . .' The ruler slipped from his grasp.

'You've visited the Poulencs' bookshop, haven't you?'

'I . . . yes.' His hands were clasped now.

'How often?'

'Once a month . . . something like that. I didn't make a tally. Kept an eye open for new stock.'

'And bought a good deal?'

'Depends on what you call a good deal. Twenty or thirty volumes over the last couple of years.'

'A fair investment.'

Gordon was sweating lightly. 'I'm a French specialist. And some of the eighteenth-century titles I wanted weren't easily come by.'

'Tried Charing Cross Road?'

'Of course. But I don't care to spend time and money chasing up to Town if I can get what I need on my door-step.'

'At a price.'

'A fair price on the whole. You pay for the convenience of a local shop. The Poulencs are in a small way. Need a decent profit margin to keep them going.'

'But they won't get it any longer, will they, Dr Gordon?'

'I'm not sure that I'm with you.'

'Oh, I think you are. The Poulencs have a room to let. Does that surprise you?'

'I know nothing about their private affairs.'

'Cheryl Hobbs's affairs weren't exactly private, were they?'

'Not any longer, it seems.' Gordon's hands sketched a gesture of surrender. 'I'd have thought Madame would have kept her mouth shut.'

'She had no choice.'

'I see. And neither do I?'

'It would make things easier.'

Armstrong turned over a page of his notebook.

'She wasn't a common prostitute, you know. Nothing common about her.'

'When did you first . . .?'

'About a year ago. Oh, I'd spoken to her four or five times before. It's a bit cramped downstairs. They have this big notice: "More stock on the first floor. Browsers welcome." First four or five visits I did just that. Cheryl hovered around the upper rooms when I was there. Made a show of dusting books or checking titles against an inventory. I didn't pay much attention. Just assumed she was keeping an eye open for shoplifters.'

'And the next time?'

'The next time was last March. I was feeling pretty lousy. Jane had taken leave to visit her mother in Stirling. Old woman was in a bad way, or so she made out. Copper-lined hypochondriac, in my judgement. Jane planned to stay up there for a week. It was the last week of Hilary Term and I couldn't get away. But when she came back the two of us were to have the next week in Auvergne. Mother-in-law stage-managed a relapse that put paid to that scheme. We had a stinker of a row over the 'phone one evening. It was the first time Jane and I'd been apart for more than a few days. And I missed her like hell. I begged her to come home but she dug her heels in. And I was damned if I'd go up there to dance attendance on the old tyrant. Next day, to put the tin lid on things, a hospital appointment letter for Jane was forwarded from the clinic. I realized she'd restarted her course of fertility treatment without telling me. I went out to console myself by blueing a royalty cheque.'

'At the Poulencs?'

'Mm. On my last visit I'd spotted a volume of Diderot's letters I was lacking. So I grabbed that first. But it didn't cost the full amount of my cheque. And I'd this childish feeling that I must spend the lot in one go. I couldn't find anything else to fit the bill. The stuff was either too pricey or outside my line of country. I began to lose interest in the books and respond to Cheryl. As I scanned the shelves on the first-floor landing she abandoned all pretence of work and watched me, crouched on the bottom step of the staircase to the floor above. She was wearing a square-necked green dress, smocked over the breasts, and red stockings. Like a girl in a Margaret Tarrant illustration. A Twenties vision of a mediaeval.

'"Not your day, is it?" she asked at last.

'"So it seems."

'"Poor you." She got up then, walked over slowly and kissed me. Then she stood back, smiling. I was just dazed at first. Plenty of girl undergrads had made a pass at me over the years, God knows. But she was different. Cool and self-possessed, and—crazy as it must sound—virginal. Then her body smell got to me. I began to shake. She can have been in no doubt of the state I was in. And, still smiling, she unfastened the top buttons of her dress. Then she turned and began to walk upstairs. And I followed her.'

There was a short silence.

'Diderot says, "There is only one virtue, justice, one duty, to be happy."'

'So you reckoned you owed yourself?' Baxter's tone was harsher than he had intended.

'Something like that.'

'And you went on seeing her?'

'Mmm. Trinity Term's always grim. So much examining and admin. And Jane was wrapped up in her own concerns. Her research was going through a sticky patch. And she was uptight about the fertility treatment. Sex was real, sex was earnest.'

'You did better with Cheryl?'

'Mm. She had the Cleopatra thing, you know . . . infinite variety. And empathy to the nth degree. But something was missing. Most men fantasize about their girlfriends when they make love to their wives. It was the other way round with me. I fantasized about Jane when I was with Cheryl.'

'When did your wife find out?' Baxter asked, recalling Jane Gordon's unease during his visit to Newnham.

'It was one afternoon in June. She came home earlier than usual—before I'd had time to shower. She smelt Cheryl's perfume.'

'And you told her?'

'Not straight away. Said I'd had an affectionate farewell from one of my students. But a week or two later she noticed the perfume on one of the books I'd bought from the Poulencs.'

'So you owned up?'

'Not quite. Told myself it was kinder to Jane to conceal the fact that Cheryl was a pro. Sparing my own pride, I dare say. Now it'll all come out, I suppose?'

'The quicker the less painful to all concerned, in my opinion. So we'd welcome your help.'

'Help?'

'Come on, Dr Gordon. You must have run into other clients.'

He shook his head. 'Pepper Street's hardly a hive of activity. And after . . . after I'd gone to bed with her Cheryl told me to come back at a fixed time. To avoid accidental encounters, I suppose.'

'I find it hard to believe you heard nothing on the grapevine. Surely some of your colleagues talked when they'd had a jar.'

Gordon grimaced. 'Sexual liberation's spawned its own taboos. With the cream of well-endowed young womanhood ready, willing and able, you don't score Brownie points in Combination Rooms for resorting to a back street whore.'

'But you must at least have an idea of the pool from which Cheryl Hobbs's clients were drawn. Scholars who patronized the shop—French specialists, for the most part, I suppose?'

'Christ, no. Just as likely to be historians, philosophers, economists. Any arts scholar worth his salt and many a scientist has a reading knowledge of several foreign languages. And you can't confine yourself to those seeking texts for their content—you'll need to add in the bibliophiles.'

'So we're talking about the whole academic community?'

'Potentially.'

'I see.' Baxter rose abruptly. 'It would seem, Dr Gordon, that we are wasting each other's time. Here's the number to ring if you recall anything more specific.

'Bastard!' Armstrong exploded as they hurried along the corridor. 'All he's worried about is his nice safe ivory tower.'

'And his wife,' Baxter added. 'I do think he might be worried about his wife. "There is only one virtue, justice".'

'Are you trying to tell me Jane Gordon might have taken the law into her own hands?'

'I'm suggesting it's a possibility we shouldn't exclude.'

They had come in a police car. As he was belting himself in, Baxter called the incidents room. His companion watched his face darken.

'Next stop Pepper Street?'

His superior nodded, reaching in his pocket for an indigestion tablet. 'Make it *vito*. *Molto* bloody *vito*.'

Ranged outside the bookshop were Detective-Sergeant Short, the police surgeon and a uniformed constable. The old woman and dog they had seen the day before stood a few yards away.

'Well, Colin?'

'PC McKinley took over from PC Hall at 5 am. You'll have seen Hall's report?'

Baxter muttered noncommitally. He had contented himself with the Duty Sergeant's summary. Like many applied scientists, he valued negative evidence more highly in theory than in practice first thing in the morning.

'Constable?'

The fairskinned lad blushed. 'Milkman called around 7.15, sir. Thought they'd have brought it in before 9.00, so I radioed DS Short. He instructed me to wait until opening time—9.30 according to the notice on the door. Still no sign of life. So I gave a ring and a good hard thump.'

'Without result?'

'Not a squeak.'

'Tried the back?'

'Mm-hmm. Yard door locked and barred.'

Baxter raised his eyes to scan the front windows of the upper storeys. His eye caught a barely visible wisp of smoke.

'They lit a fire.'

'Last night around nine, sir,' Short informed him. 'It was in Hall's report.'

And nobody had thought fit to tell him. For crying out loud. But then again why should they?

'Break down the door.' He turned up his coat collar against the sharp breeze and waited.

Five minutes later they made their way through the darkened shop to the room behind. Marie Poulenc had composed her husband's body in some semblance of dignity. He sat in his usual chair, head drooping but hands folded neatly. Her own body sprawled half-kneeling on the floor beside him. Her head, tied into the plastic shopping-bag that had probably served them both, still lay in Jean-Claude's lap. But the hand that seemed to have been clasping his had lost its grip and lay helpless, its ring-claws caught in the rug around the dead man's knees.

After a cursory glance at the charred fragments of paper in the grate, Baxter turned to the open roll-top desk. As he had surmised, the pigeon-holes were now completely empty. Two empty wine glasses stood on the dining-table, together with a pile of three books and an open medal box containing a Croix de Guerre. Handwritten cards indicated the legatees of books and medal. Stooping and squinting to read the shaky script, the Chief Inspector learnt that the morocco-bound volumes, described as the work of the Comte de Caumont, were intended to augment the collection of his bindings in the Fitzwilliam Museum. 'The work of one French *émigré*, the gift of a second. In gratitude to the University and City of Cambridge.' On the second card was written 'To Charles Poulenc' and a Paris address.

'The son, I suppose,' said Armstrong, reading over his shoulder. 'Did the decent thing in the end, didn't they? You can't help admiring them.'

For closing the circle? A nice little, tight little bourgeois family circle that effectively excluded their second-floor ghost and her living child. Ill-disposed to stand and stare, Baxter left Armstrong to summon the scene-of-crime specialists. As he stepped into the cold street he brought up a bellyful of gas. The indigestion tablet had done a good short-term job on his stomach acids but nothing for his frustration.

Across the street the doors of the garage stood open. An Asian boy in new, overlarge dungarees lay on his back beneath a Triumph Herald. A haggard man in late middle-age was spraying a Mini. Behind them he could see a higgledy-piggledy collection of body parts. Envying their purposeful absorption in the task in hand, he summoned PC McKinley to drive him back to Holtchester. Once in his office, he forced himself to concentrate on routine administrative work for two solid hours before masticating an early lunch with all the care that his doctor had recommended and setting off on his afternoon's business.

CHAPTER 11

'My object all sublime
I shall achieve in time—
To let the punishment fit the crime,
The punishment fit the crime.'

'No, no lad.' A petulant speaking voice interrupted the bass-baritone. 'Spit out the bubblegum. Let's hear those unvoiced consonants. Puh! Tuh! Again:

'To *let* the *pun*ishment *fit* the crime,
The *pun*ishment *fit* the crime.'

How neat and tidy it sounded. Baxter squirmed as the lyrics floated into the stationery cupboard that served as a general office at Browne Community College. The plump typist, whose knees brushed his, had no idea where the Acting Head might be. She could, however, offer some guesses as to the whereabouts of her senior, the Acting Head's secretary, and had sent a prefect in her pursuit.

There was a rap at the hatch. It was Armstrong, red-faced and breathless. The Chief Inspector went out into the corridor to speak to him.

'Complications?'

'Nope. Two clear sets of prints—and some of Marie's were sooty. Looks as though she helped the old boy on his way before burning the papers and doing herself in. They're trawling the locality, of course, but I doubt if the neighbours will have much to say. Not that they had any close neighbours.'

'Except the garage.'

'Oh yes?'

But before he could elaborate his hunch the Chief Inspector was greeted by a brisk, curly-haired woman bearing a box marked with a red cross.

'Sorry about this! Hope you like G and S. No rest for the wicked. Never leave the office unattended as a rule. But we'd a minicrisis in the gym when Sandra—my assistant— was on lunch, and I was the only First Aider on call. Minor nosebleed as it turned out, but some kids panic at the sight of blood.'

'Not just kids, Mrs . . .'

'Wallace. Viv Wallace.' She inspected the proffered card. 'But you'd know all about that, Chief Inspector. How can I help you?'

'We were hoping to see Mr Henderson.'

'You're out of luck, I suspect.' She reached a muscular arm through the hatch for a desk diary. 'Mm. Thought as much. No appointments before 2.30—he's taking a long lunch break at home.'

'Lucky man.'

'Oh, it'll be a working lunch, I assure you. Mrs Henderson's up to her eyes in school affairs—they make a marvellous team. Things are particularly hectic this week with *The Mikado* on Thursday and Friday and the Sports Gala on Saturday.'

'I can imagine.'

'Will you wait?' Viv Wallace asked, against renewed competition from the bass-baritone.

Baxter consulted his watch. 2.15. 'No, thanks. We'll nip

round to the house. I know the address.' No point in asking
her not to ring. She had the air of a woman with well-
developed protective instincts. The two men walked briskly
down the corridor, pursued by the chirrups of the Three
Little Maids:

> 'Everything is a source of fun,
> Nobody's safe, for we care for none!
> Life is a joke that's just begun!'

Baxter let the glass door bang behind him. 'Jesus Christ!'
'Easy on,' said Armstrong. 'Don't take it out on G and S.
Some catchy tunes in that show.'
'Perhaps they should try listening to the words before
they din them into the heads of the young.' But he was less
disturbed by the words they had just heard than by another
fragment of libretto that hovered tantalizingly just beyond
recall.

'In you come, girls. The door's on the latch.'
'Mrs Henderson?' The policemen had circumnavigated a
blue Toyota to reach the doorstep of the detached brick
villa. An untidy, bespectacled woman in her late thirties
came out to greet them. A measuring tape hung round her
neck and there were several dozen pins stuck in her padded
jacket. Behind her, brightly coloured garments were draped
over banisters and overflowing from cardboard cartons.
'Yes, I'm Louise Henderson. Awfully sorry. I'm expecting
some friends from the PTA.' Her smile faded as she read
the identity card.
'We've come to see your husband.'
'You've missed him by five minutes, I'm afraid. His
secretary rang to say someone would be calling round to see
him—she didn't give your name . . .'
'She wouldn't, would she?' Baxter's face crinkled. 'Mrs
Wallace struck me as the discreet type.'

She smiled a quick, schoolgirlish smile. 'Viv's very loyal. But in any case John couldn't have waited. I'm using the car this afternoon to transport costumes. He had to give himself twenty minutes to walk back to school.'

'Then perhaps we could have a word with you, Mrs Henderson, in view of your involvement with the Parent-Teachers Association. We're investigating the murder of a pupil's mother.'

'That poor Hobbs woman.' Louise Henderson's sensitive mouth quivered briefly. 'Come in if you wish, but I'm afraid there's not much I can tell you.' She led the way through a large hall, pausing at the open door of the lounge where a dark-haired girl was machining. 'You'd better come through to the breakfast room. Rosemary will answer the door, won't you, love?'

A pile of foil-covered Japanese swords occupied a considerable share of the floorspace in the small, square room they entered.

'An action-packed week, I gather. You'll be glad of your half-term holiday?'

'You can say that again. I'm trying hard not to let the Christmas panto and carol services cast their shadows before.'

'Meanwhile *The Mikado*. Are you a Gibert and Sullivan fan yourself?'

'Not really. John and I would have preferred something more meaningful . . . more accessible to the kids. But the Governors love G and S. So do some of the pushier parents. And it's hardly the time . . .' She blushed, as if for the indiscretion, which Baxter pretended not to notice.

'And you're Wardrobe Mistress?'

'Oh no. John and I don't think it's a good idea for a teacher's wife to run PTA shows even if she is a parent. But we're relatively near the school and we've plenty of space so working parties tend to meet here.'

From the wicker chairs to which she had ushered them

the detectives had a close-up view of a hessian screen covered with snapshots of adults and children.

'You must have got to know a lot of parents over the years,' Armstrong observed.

'Stacks. Browne's a real community school. Our parents have been very forthcoming.'

'Including Cheryl Hobbs?'

Louise Henderson shook her head. 'Cheryl was one of my failures. John says I'm silly to think of it like that, but I can't help it. Not that we could have made any difference in the long run . . .' Her voice trailed away.

'You did meet her, then?' Baxter asked, signalling to his colleague his intention of taking up the questioning.

'Oh yes. John had overall responsibility for pastoral work before he became Acting Head. And he took special trouble with the parents of children with problems—Martin Hobbs was a school refuser. Had them round to our house once a term—more often when they were going through a bad patch. I got involved because I was teaching Art at the time. Most kids can do something in the Art line if you give them their head and the rudiments of a technique. So I could prove to parents like Cheryl Hobbs that their kids were functioning adequately in some areas even if they were grossly incompetent in others.'

'But Mrs Hobbs didn't appreciate the demonstration?'

'Evidently not. She came to the house once and never again. I felt guilty, because I had been so sorry for her.'

'Oh?'

'She was prickly. I got the impression that she didn't trust other women—and I could understand that. If only I'd told her . . .'

'Told her what?'

'That I knew what it felt like to be a single parent. I had my twins at Art School—a pretty tolerant environment. But when I'd qualified and started teaching it was a different story. I was sinking for the third time when I met John . . .'

She shivered. 'Wasting your time, aren't I? Sorry about that. There's nothing useful I can tell you about Cheryl Hobbs. My husband may know a little more, but I doubt it.'

Baxter got up from his creaking chair. 'We can only try.'

His eye caught a group of figurines on a high shelf. 'Bronze?'

'Fibreglass.'

'May I?' His hand hovered over the paired figures, almost identical in babyhood but individualized by age and sex as they progressed to sturdy adolescence.

'Your boy and girl. Do they go to Browne?'

'Till this year. They've started sixth-form college.'

'Your son's a diver?' Baxter picked up a sculpture set a little way apart from the others. The style was formal, the facial features undefined. But there was something about the set of the bent head that struck him as familiar.

'Oh, that's not Robbie. It's my husband's brother—done from a photograph. Not a great success, I'm afraid.'

He replaced the piece on the shelf. 'Good for the moral fibre, they say, confronting one's failures.'

'But never easy.' Her voice faltered on the last word.

She followed them to the door. The dark-haired girl in the lounge had acquired two chattering companions.

'Mrs Tomlinson found the body, I believe. How ghastly for her.'

Baxter paused on the doorstep.

'You know Mrs Tomlinson?'

'Slightly.' Louise Henderson hesitated. 'She helped me professionally once, long ago. A kind woman. A kind, wise woman.'

The detectives noticed with surprise that her eyes were full of tears.

'Please make yourselves comfortable.' The school secretary scooped up the contents of the Acting Head's out-tray. 'Mr

Henderson asked me to say he'd be with you very shortly.'
She hurried away, leaving the door of the Head's office ajar.
The left-hand section of a wallboard running the length of
one wall was occupied by a time-table of daunting com-
plexity, the right-hand section by a wall-planner. It was the
latter that attracted both men's attention.

'All go this term,' said Armstrong.

'And half-term.' Baxter's finger indicated entries in three
or four coded colours for the following week and returned
to linger over Wednesday, where several jottings had
been overwritten by the single word 'Interview' in block
capitals.

'He'll be glad to get that over,' Armstrong observed.

'Oh?'

'Interview for the Headship. Haven't you heard? Hot
local issue. Been lots of chat about it down in HQ.'

Armstrong picked up such snippets in the cafeteria, where
his senior rarely lingered.

'So that's why his wife didn't want to rock the Governors'
boat. What are Henderson's chances?'

'God knows. Most of the locals are rooting for him, but
the post should attract a big field.'

'Impressed?' The big man smiled as they swivelled round
to face him. 'Whatever did we do without these gimmicks
to advertise our busyness?'

Baxter strove to dispel irrational stirrings of schoolboy
guilt as he settled into one of the easy chairs facing the desk.
Henderson with his clean-cut features and athletic physique
took the Headmaster's seat with every appearance of relaxed
authority.

'I don't need persuading that an Acting Headship is a
job and a half,' Baxter retorted, deciding that there was
little to be lost in a frontal assault. 'You'll be glad to be shot
of it?'

Henderson hesitated briefly. 'It'll be a relief to have the
business settled. For me, for the school.'

'Then may I wish you good luck . . . assuming you want the job?'

'Let's say that after ten years' hard slog I shouldn't like to see the post go to someone wildly unsuitable.'

'Understandable. As you've presumably been told, we're here in connection with a murder.'

'I know.' Henderson straightened some papers before resuming eye contact. 'Poor Mrs Hobbs. Poor Martin.' He sighed. 'I'm a doer by nature. Believe most problems can be solved by getting the finger out. Then this sort of thing comes along—wham! And leaves you feeling so bloody helpless.'

'You were personally involved with the family?'

'No more than with several others. Martin was one of a half-dozen or so in his peer group who needed extra attention. Especially during his first year.'

'He was having treatment, wasn't he?'

'Human resources therapy? Well, yes. Doesn't do any harm, I daresay, but in our experience it doesn't do much good either. Holtchester's a far cry from turn-of-the-century Vienna, but the child guidance crowd don't seem to want to know about our real problems.'

'Such as?'

'Drug abuse for one. We wanted a psychiatric rep on our local working party. Peter Denny looked like the obvious choice but he turned the invitation down flat.'

'The Hobbs weren't into drugs, were they?'

'Lord, no. Martin's problem was pretty simple really, whatever the HRT team would have you believe.'

'Oh, yes?'

'Hadn't learnt how to cope with bullies—lack of male models in his early years. Common enough among fatherless boys.'

'Smother-loved, would you say?'

'*No!*' Henderson rejected the term with a force that disrupted the easy instructional flow of his discourse. But only momentarily. 'Mrs Hobbs may have been somewhat inconsistent in her management of the boy. But she wasn't overprotective.'

'Except in relation to his father?'

'Perhaps.' Henderson's broad, freckled wrist rotated outwards in a gesture of concession. 'She felt that Hobbs wanted custody rather than access. Give him an inch, she reckoned, and he'd take an ell. She may well have been right. Steve Hobbs had an obsession about his son. Used to hang around the school gates trying to intercept him till I warned him off. Boy's scared stiff of him.'

'Perhaps Mrs Hobbs felt she could do better for the lad —provide him with a more satisfactory father?'

'I'm not with you, I'm afraid.'

By your own choice, Baxter surmised, recognizing behind the expression of frank perplexity a mask as professional as his own. 'She was planning to remarry. Didn't you know?'

'I wouldn't expect to, unless it was public knowledge. Come to think of it, I only spoke to the woman once during the present school year.'

'When was that?'

'Just a sec. I keep a record of home visits.' He flicked back through the pages of a well-filled desk diary. 'Ah yes. Third Tuesday in September. New form, new form master, new curriculum. Martin was panicking. Fairly regular phenomenon for kids with a history of school refusal. Picked him up at his home myself and had a brief chat with Mrs Hobbs.'

'Sort everything out then and there?'

'More or less.' Henderson riffled through a few more pages. 'I drove Martin to school every morning that week. But on the Wednesday, Thursday and Friday his mother had left the house before I had arrived. I decided he could manage on his own after that—and he did.'

'And you had no further contact with Mrs Hobbs this term? Quite sure?'

'Positive. Matter of policy, really. The year counsellors take major responsibility for contacting parents, and by and large I let them get on with it. Not that the second-year counsellor had much joy with Mrs H. She told him she saw no point in visiting the school now Martin had settled down. Pity, really. The lad needed encouragement. I almost rang her myself on Thursday evening to urge her to attend the Sports Gala.'

'Almost?'

'The boy told me she wouldn't be at home . . . she'd be at the guidance clinic.'

'Ring her there?'

Henderson shook his head. 'Thought I might be intruding . . . that she'd probably gone to keep an appointment with the social worker. The typewriter story sounded rather farfetched.'

'Were you angry?'

'*Angry?*' The question had evidently touched a nerve.

'That Mrs Hobbs should choose to confide in a professional other than you or your colleague.'

'Oh, that. Professional jealousy.' Henderson relaxed visibly, permitting himself a rueful smile. 'Could have been, if I'm honest. Disappointed, anyhow. But then I couldn't be sure.'

'You were working late that evening?'

'As usual when the youth club's in action. One of my special interests.'

'How late?'

'Nine-thirty . . . quarter to ten. Couldn't be precise.'

'Can you remember where you went after you spoke to Martin Hobbs?'

'To this office. The school timetable should have been settled by the beginning of the month, but our software package developed a few bugs, so it turned out to be a pencil-and-rubber job. I was determined to finalize it before half-term.'

'So you stayed in this room till nine-thirty at least?'

'Not constantly, no. Don't like to be deskbound for too long. Besides, I wanted to check up on some maintenance work. Like to make sure the place is in good order for our public functions.'

'Ah, yes.' Baxter got to his feet. 'Quite a week for you, isn't it?'

'For the school,' Henderson corrected him, rising from the chair for which he was bidding.

'Decent fellow,' Armstrong observed, as the policemen crossed the leaf-strewn playground.'

'On the surface.'

'Oh, come off it. You need more than veneer to build up a school the way he has. Browne has came up from pretty near the bottom of the comprehensive league by all accounts. And the locals give a lot of the credit to Henderson.'

'Oh, I don't doubt the man has leadership potential.'

'And his wife seems devoted. Did you notice that "John and I" stuff?'

Baxter laughed. 'Envious? And without cause, I'd guess. Togetherness can become a mite claustrophobic.'

'You don't think . . .?'

'I don't know. For Christ's sake, man. I don't know.' He eased himself into the front passenger seat of Armstrong's car, snapped tight his safety belt and waited.

'Where now?' the other man asked, ignoring the outburst.

'The station. We'll have to talk to Martin's little chum —Susie Whatsername?'

'Forbes.'

'—But we'd better tackle her on her home ground after school.' An hour's hard, undisturbed thought in the privacy of his office was his immediate imperative.

Armstrong had another, suppressed until the two men stood inside the headquarters building, awaiting the lift.

'Something's been bugging me. Maybe it's nonsense . . .'

'All the more reason to get it out of your mental baggage compartment.'

'It's something I need to show you. Stuff's in my office.'

Groaning inwardly, the Chief Inspector followed him along the third floor corridor. Armstrong selected a folder from his desk drawer and spread the contents over the working surface.

'Clinic medicine cupboard.'

'So I see. Denny had the only keys, hadn't he?'

'That's what they said.'

'And he dispensed codeine on Thursday morning?'

'Right.'

'So what's your problem? Haven't found any other finger-prints, have they?'

'Nope.'

'Well, then?' Baxter thought longingly of a fragrant cup of Orange Pekoe.

'Have a look at this pic.'

Baxter squinted at a shot of the open cupboard and its undisturbed contents. 'Everything shipshape and Bristol fashion.'

'But to judge by his desk drawers Denny wasn't a tidy man.'

'Not when he didn't have to be, perhaps. But doctors are trained to be careful with drugs. Negligence can be pricey.'

'True.'

'Besides, the prints look OK.' Baxter inspected the blow-ups. 'Several good clear sets, including the codeine bottle. And the odd bit of smudging that you'd expect.'

'That's what I thought—at first. Then I noticed these.' Armstrong's horizontal ballpoint hovered over a series of white lines showing below the caps of several larger bottles. 'Let's blow it up a bit more.' He positioned a magnifying-glass over the prints.

'My God, yes. Tweezers?'

'Looks like it, doesn't it? Looks as though someone shifted several bottles and repositioned them.'

'You're bloody right, Bill.'

'A careful operator. After something specific. Anxious to cover up his tracks.'

'Or hers. No smudges on the handles, I see.'

'Could have opened the two cupboard doors by pulling on the keys.'

'Denny's set? But he had them on him on Friday.'

Baxter shrugged. 'Likely as not. But he left the bunch lying around now and then. Anyone on the clinic staff could have had them copied.'

'Cheryl Hobbs? She'd have had dealings with keys in the hotel trade.'

And drugs? Baxter wrestled again with the unfinished sentence in Hilde Tomlinson's casenotes.

'Could have been the boy,' Armstrong continued. 'He must have had plenty of opportunities to study Denny's habits. These disturbed kids can be cunning.'

'No end of possibilities, is there? The mind boggles.'

Armstrong recognized sadly but with little surprise that his superior's immediate concern was his position in the queue for tea.

'I don't know, I'm sure. What do you say, George?' Vera Forbes, a thinner, more anxious version of her daughter, glanced sideways at her husband.

'Don't see as we've any option. You'll go easy with her, Inspector?'

'You'll be there to make sure we do,' Baxter pointed out. 'But we need Susie's help.'

'All right then.' Forbes opened the door of a neat lounge and jerked his head. 'In you go. Nothing to be frightened of, Sue, if you answer the gentlemen's questions.'

His heartiness lacked conviction, but Susie, dishevelled and glowing, showed little sign of anxiety as she withdrew from a tussle with a spaniel puppy and perched on the arm of her mother's chair.

'We'd like to ask you about last Thursday evening,' Baxter began.

'About Martin? I wanted to come to the police station but Mum and Dad wouldn't let me. Soon as I heard you'd been talking to Dave Wright. He's got it in for Martin, you know. Especially since he's taken a fancy to me, the big slob.'

'Susie!'

'Well, it's true, Dad. And if it's true, I have to say it, don't I? Like you told me.'

'You only have to answer their questions.'

Susie tossed her head and stared at the Chief Inspector.

'You think Martin did it, don't you?'

'No.'

'You must do, or you wouldn't have had him put away. Where have they taken him?'

'To a children's home in Norfolk. Lovely place, they tell me. Lovely grounds.'

'Not so lovely if your mother's just been murdered and you're miles away from anyone you know.' The girl's black eyes maintained their accusing gaze.

'It's only a temporary arrangement, Susie. For his own safety.'

'Safety?' Her voice faltered.

'Martin caught a glimpse of the murderer. And the murderer probably knows that. Realizes that as soon as he gets over the shock Martin may remember something that will incriminate him . . . or her.'

'Oh, my God.' Susie covered her mouth with her hand and began to weep.

'You didn't have to tell her that,' George Forbes growled. 'You didn't have to frighten her.'

'I'm afraid we did, Mr Forbes. Your daughter's not a baby and it wouldn't have been kind to have kept her in the dark. Truth is less frightening than a nightmare.'

'I'm all right, Dad.' Susie blew her nose. 'Have you got Martin's address? Can I write to him?'

'Of course. Inspector Armstrong's writing is clearer than mine.'

'I don't know that I want Susie to be involved . . .' Vera Forbes began, as Armstrong handed over the address.

'Boy hasn't done anything wrong, according to the Chief Inspector,' her husband cut in. 'Never saw much harm in him, poor little bastard, whatever the mother may have been.'

'Can we get back to Thursday, Susie?' Baxter resumed. 'Dave Wright said Martin was buying earrings for his mother. Is that true?'

Susie nodded.

'Can you tell me about those earrings? Anything special about them?'

'They were in the shape of little leaves—beech leaves. A replacement for a pair Martin had given her in the summer, but those were oak leaves, I think. We take the casts from real leaves, tiny ones. We collect them at Chess Wood when we visit the school Outdoor Pursuits Centre.'

'You go there for Natural History classes?'

'Environmental studies, they call it,' she corrected him. 'It's all sorts of things rolled into one. Part of the time you can choose what you want to do. Martin and I mostly choose sketching. Our form went there eight or nine afternoons last spring and for a whole week in June. It was great. Martin was a bit panicky at times, but he loved it in the end. First time he'd slept away from home, except at his auntie's. Some of the parents came to visit, but Martin's mum couldn't.'

'Or wouldn't,' George Forbes growled.

'Don't be like that, Dad. Mrs Hobbs was all right. Martin wouldn't have thought so much of her otherwise, would he?'

'I daresay not, love.' Vera Forbes shot her husband a warning glance. 'Any more questions, Chief Inspector?'

'Not many. How did Martin behave on Thursday evening, Susie? How did he seem in himself?'

'Excited at first. He'd worked hard on his trampoline routine and he was over the moon about being in the display team. And he was all worked up about giving his Mum the surprise present. But then . . .'

'Then?'

'Dave Wright barged in and spoilt everything. Oh, he was just showing off, but he was really horrid. Hinted that Mrs Hobbs slept around and said she was very careless to have lost the first pair of earrings.'

'How did Martin take that?'

'He was terribly upset. Angry, but upset as well. It seemed to get him where it hurt. I wished he'd slap Dave in the face, but he didn't. He just flushed up and I thought he was going to burst into tears. But he took to his heels instead and rushed out of the room. I could hear him thumping all the way down the corridor.'

'Did you guess he was going to the clinic?'

She shook her head. 'Hadn't said a word about that. He was always a bit embarrassed about going to child guidance. Reckoned it was babyish.'

'Martin had been excited about something else recently, hadn't he? Didn't he think he'd found out the name of his real father?'

She nodded, fiddling with the pleats of her red miniskirt.

'Did he say you were the only person he'd told?'

She nodded again, biting her full lower lip.

'Who was it?'

'I'm not telling. Martin can tell you if he wants—it's his secret. You can ask me till you're blue in the face but I'm not telling.'

'Maybe it's for the boy's good, Susie,' George Forbes said gently.

'It's Martin's secret,' she insisted, chin lifted.

'That's all right, Susie,' said Baxter.

'She may think different when she's slept on it,' Vera

Forbes suggested as she saw them off at the front door.

'I doubt it. Anyhow, don't lean on her. Let it go.'

The transforming powers of sleep never failed to surprise and mildly alarm the Chief Inspector. He awoke in the small hours of the next morning, haunted by a rediscovered tune, and found no rest till he had pieced together the half-remembered lyrics.

> There is beauty in the bellow of the blast,
> There is grandeur in the growling of the gale
> There is eloquent outpouring
> When the lion is a-roaring
> And the tiger is a-lashing of his tail.
> Yes I like to see a tiger
> From the Congo or the Niger,
> And especially when lashing of his tail!

The words had terrified him on first hearing in a D'Oyly Carte production of *The Mikado* to which he had been taken as a ninth birthday treat. They frightened him more than a little now.

CHAPTER 12

'Why Cambridge?' Armstrong asked, wiping the inside of an already clear windscreen. It was nine o'clock on Tuesday morning.

'Why not Peter Denny?' Baxter snapped his seat-belt. 'That what you mean, Bill?'

'Right. Why not shove the drugs cupboard evidence under his nose and Hilde Tomlinson's? You're not trying to tell me it's not important?'

'No. But I'm saying it's messy.' Messy enough to concern

Superintendent Caskey, perhaps. 'And the CC wants a clean job. A nice, quick, clean job. We'll go back to Denny and Tomlinson if we have to. But I've a hunch we might save ourselves time and trouble by another trip to Pepper Street.'

All the same, he had taken care to keep his communication channels open, choosing to travel in the police Vauxhall and switching on his personal bleeper.

'How many?' The young Asian mechanic smiled through the car window.

'No petrol, thanks. But we'd appreciate a word with your boss.'

'Half a sec.'

A small man, muffled beneath his khaki overalls, emerged from the half-open door of the garage. One gulp of raw air and he subsided in a fit of coughing.

'Mr Leslie Witcham?'

It was several seconds before the garage owner could do more than nod and smile.

'Spare a few minutes? Want us to park inside? Looks as though we're blocking your pumps out here.'

'You're welcome.' Another fit of coughing. 'Open up, Ahmed.' There was just enough room for the Vauxhall in the modestly equipped workshop. The Triumph Herald he had noticed yesterday had disappeared, but the Mini awaited its final coat. A ten-year-old Hillman Minx stood on a single-post lift and a rusting Austin Princess lurked in a corner. The back door of the workshop opened on to a small yard containing a heap of scrap and a couple of partly dismantled chassis. The garage owner waved them in the direction of a small makeshift office and the warmth of an electric fire.

'Nasty cough, Mr Witcham,' Baxter observed. 'Sounds as though you ought to be in bed.'

'No rest for the wicked, Chief Inspector.' Witcham wheezed gently as he peered at his visitors' credentials. 'Not

for the self-employed wicked, anyroads. Sit yourselves down
and tell me what I can do for you. You won't mind if I take
a swig of the old lemon and glycerine while you're at it?'

He poured himself a cupful of yellow liquid from a
Thermos. 'Nothing like it for the Cambridge chest.'

Baxter announced his purpose with atypical lack of
conviction. Death seemed far removed from the cheerful
jumble of this cosy office. Walls and windows were so heavily
plastered with ageing advertisements and pricelists as
almost to exclude the view of the petrol pumps and beyond
them the opposite side of Pepper Street.

But Witcham, sipping his medicine with evident relish,
showed no surprise at the statement.

'Bad business, isn't it? I've read the papers, of course.
And your men have been round. Nothing much I could tell
them, though. Or you, if Hardy comes to Hardy. I knew
the Poulencs by sight but not to speak to. Same goes for her
. . . Mrs Hobbs. People don't bother with each other round
this way. Didn't even know her name till I read it in the
News. The Poulencs drove Renaults. Mrs P stopped here for
petrol once in a blue moon but we didn't do anything else
for her. Far as I know, Mrs Hobbs didn't drive.'

'But her ex-husband did.'

'Steve? Yeah.' Witcham made a business of replacing the
plastic cup on his flask.

'Mate of yours?'

'Manner of speaking.' He coughed voluntarily, loosely,
hawked and blew his nose. 'Sorry.'

'Known him a long time?'

'Fourteen—fifteen years off and on. Lost touch when he
went bust and moved out of the county.'

'And during that time he never introduced you to his wife
. . . ex-wife?'

'Never.'

'You surprise me.'

The small man shrugged. 'Didn't bother me. Missus and

I have never been ones for socializing. And Steve can't have had much time for it once he got started on his own. He was aiming high in those days. Put body and soul into the business, I reckon. Besides, we were living in Cambridge and the Hobbses were in Holtchester.'

'But not for long.'

'No. Steve's bankruptcy was public knowledge, of course. But he never talked about his private life in those days. Didn't hear about the divorce for some months after he'd gone to London.'

'When did he come your way again?'

Witcham looked uneasy.

'Where's all this leading, Chief Inspector? Steve Hobbs is a decent lad. I'd trust him with my life. He'd no part in that trouble across the road—I'd take an oath on it.'

'We know that.'

'As for her . . . that Cheryl. I don't suppose he'd any idea she worked there. She went out and about a bit but never at lunchtimes. And like I said, I couldn't have put a name to her.'

'When did Hobbs show up again?' Baxter persisted.

'Two to two-and-a-half years ago. Summer it was, June or July. Seemed more sure of himself, somehow. Said he'd remarried. Paid off his creditors and slapped down a big deposit on a bungalow at Maryham.'

'Was this just a social visit?'

'No. Steve had kept his hand in the car business. Buying up old bangers at auctions and tarting them up. But he hadn't the space or the tools for the job at home.'

'So he asked for your help. Why you?'

'Knew the smart outfits wouldn't give him houseroom, I suppose. Stands to reason. I haven't the physique for the rat-race myself. Or the inclination. Business is pretty slow here, but overheads are low, and I've built up a useful collection of spares over the years. Needed sorting out, and Steve offered to put it in order for me. Deal was that he

could take any spares he needed for free and make use of
my premises and equipment.'

'Nice deal for him.'

'Oh, it was worth it to get the stock sorted. Most customers
don't want to scrabble through a scrapheap these days.
Don't know what they're bloody well looking for unless
you've labelled it. Besides, Steve minded the shop for me
now and then.'

'He'd time on his hands?'

'Two or three hours in the middle of the day when he was
on the split shift. Other drivers didn't like it, so he'd often
do a swop. Suited him to have the free time in daylight. And
it suited me to get away from the place every so often.
Collecting and delivering, visiting wholesalers, that sort of
thing. Ahmed's a bright boy, but he's under driving age,
and I promised his dad I'd never leave him on his own.
There have been one or two incidents round here . . .'

'What was Hobbs usually doing when you came back to
the garage?'

'Working—he's a hard worker, Steve. Drilling, lubricat-
ing, spraying, sorting out my latest pile of scrap.'

A mechanic in mechanic's overalls—about his normal
work in his normal habitat. A familiar figure. An invisible
figure.

'Has he been round this past week?'

Witcham shook his head. 'Can't blame him, can you?
Reckon he hasn't the stomach for it, after the shock he's
had. And you know, ever since you've been here, I've been
wondering . . .'

'What?'

'Whether he did know she was working over there.
Whether he came here to be near her. Whether he still loved
her . . .'

'You hated her, didn't you?' Armstrong was struck by the
unusual severity of his senior's tone, by the set lines round

Baxter's finely carved mouth. The detectives faced Steve
Hobbs across an interrogation room in the police station at
Holtchester.

'No, I wouldn't say that.' The fat man sat forward, arms
folded on the table. 'She wasn't important enough for that.
I didn't hate her any more than I hate a garden pest.'

'That you could get rid of?'

'Could if I had to. But in Cheryl's case that would have
been crazy. It would have scarred Martin for life. I'm no
shrink but I could see that clearly enough.'

'So you spied on her?'

'Did Les . . .?'

'We've spoken to Witcham . . . and to Ahmed.'

True to the letter, if not the spirit, Armstrong reminded
his queasy conscience, scribbling down Baxter's statement.

'Lad spotted my notebook, I suppose,' Hobbs muttered,
as if drawing inspiration from the act. 'Old Les wouldn't,
not in a month of Sundays.'

'Hand it over.'

The thick fingers fumbled in an inside pocket.

Baxter scanned the pages. No shorthand here, but neat,
small script. The notes were a mixture of dates, times,
physical descriptions and initials. Not many initials.

'How many did you identify?'

'Half a dozen . . . not good going but it was difficult.
Most of them had no cars, only bikes. You have to get pretty
close to identify a grotty Cambridge bike.'

'What were you after? Blackmail?'

Hobbs flushed. 'I haven't sunk so low. Besides, what
could I get out of that lot? Most of them looked half skint.
Young dons and the like. Shouldn't think they'd much left
out of the paypacket after Cheryl and the Poulencs had
taken their whack. Oh, they bought books all right. Done
up in brown paper bags. I used to wonder about those
books.'

'What were you after?'

Hobbs clenched a pudgy fist. 'What in Christ's name do you think?'

'Custody?'

He nodded, fighting for control.

So Cheryl had been right on that score.

'Once I found out she'd been on the game I was set on it. Hit me between the eyes, it did. Hadn't a clue where she was working when I first looked up old Les. Freda may have mentioned the Poulencs but one bookshop's the same as another as far as I'm concerned. And for weeks on end I saw no sign of her in Pepper Street. Just the blokes. Couldn't help noticing the blokes. Same ones at the same time. Every week or every fortnight.

'"What kind of outfit is that?" I asked Ahmed one lunchtime.

'"Bookshop," he said, "*French* bookshop." And gave me a funny look. If Les had been around I might have asked him more. Didn't want to put ideas into the kid's head—these Pakis are particular about that sort of thing. Besides, something was ticking away at the back of my mind. That evening I went over to Freda Taylor's to check out Cheryl's employers.'

'And you bought the notebook?'

'Yep. Seemed it was all meant to be—predestined if you like. Reckoned I'd got Cheryl in the hollow of my hand as far as any sane magistrate was concerned. But I had to be sure. It was slow work, tracking those guys to their college rooms or their digs. Checking out porters' lists. And all the time I was stringing Freda along. Making her think that access was all I was interested in.'

'Why didn't you consult a solicitor?'

'Had to make sure things couldn't misfire—just had to be. Besides, I wanted to wait till Martin had settled down a bit. The child guidance business scared me. The court would probably hush up the sordid details, but saying goodbye to Mum was going to be tough on him, whatever way you looked at it.'

'Quite.' The Chief Inspector's tone retained its cutting edge. 'If the boy's welfare is your chief concern, I'm surprised you didn't come forward with this evidence before today.' He tapped the notebook. 'One of these men may have been the murderer. And your son may be his next victim.'

Hobbs sighed. 'They don't matter.'

'You've no right to jump to conclusions,' Armstrong objected.

'No right to play your little game? Perhaps not. But you know and I know, Chief Inspector, that the only one that matters is the one she was going to marry.'

'Because he found out?' The cutting edge was sheathed now, the tone silky.

'I reckon.'

'Because you told him?'

'Bloody right I would have, if I'd known who he was.'

'The marriage would have wrecked your appeal.'

'If he was a respectable type, yes. So I needed to get in first. Put the evidence in front of him, threaten to sell it to the Sundays with the information on his own involvement if he didn't back down.'

'Who was he?'

Armstrong noted the flickering eyelids, the brief hesitation.

'Freda thought he lived in London. Something to do with antiques. I wasn't so sure. But I went up to Town by Cheryl's train a couple of Sundays. Lost her the first time. Second time was just over three weeks ago. Trailed her to a shop in Kensington.'

'Belonging to a Mr Peregrine Winterson?'

' 'Sright. They spent most of the day there. Went out to a flash Knightsbridge restaurant for dinner.'

'You too?'

Hobbs laughed. 'Pretty near broke the bank over that little outing. And all for nix. Couldn't get close enough to hear what they were saying. But they didn't act like lovers to my way of thinking. Didn't look as though they were on the brink of getting spliced.'

'Any other leads?'

'Came to conclusion that the bloke she was going to marry was the one she met on Thursday afternoons.'

'Every Thursday?'

'Couldn't swear to that. Couldn't tail them every week. It meant a trip to Holtchester—getting enough time off from work. But I made it four times all told before . . . before she was killed.'

'What did he look like, this man?'

'Dunno—that's the hell of it. Had to keep my distance. There's not much cover round Cheryl's place. And she was clever. Left her house on the bike around 2.15. But she took a different route each week. She'd park the bike and go into a shop—not always the same shop. Then he'd pick her up.'

'And you didn't get so much as a glimpse?' Armstrong sneered.

Hobbs's heavy face flushed. 'I had to be careful, didn't I?'

'Car number?'

'Too many parked between us. All I know for sure is the make and colour. It was a red Maestro.'

'Are you listening?' Armstrong addressed the Chief Inspector's broad back. Baxter had carried the cup of coffee upon which he had insisted to the window of his office.

'Of course, Bill.'

'Then why don't you react when I remind you that Peter Denny drives a red Maestro?'

'Popular car, popular colour.'

'But none of our other known suspects . . .'

'All right, all right, Bill. We might be on to our man.
But let's tread gently. You were all for waving the drugs
cupboard prints in front of him, remember. Now, we carry
more clout. But we still need a strategy. Bloody hell! Answer
that 'phone, will you?' He sipped his drink, staring unseeing
at the window of the office opposite.

'Incidents room. They've got a Mrs Yvonne Chandler.
Can we spare the time to see her?'

'Depends . . . Who is she?'

'Waitress at the Ruffled Feathers.'

'Oh, we can, Bill. I certainly think we can.'

'Well?' Armstrong knew from the harshness of his superior's
bark that he was attracted by the new arrival. Girl might
be a creature from outer space with her metallic wedges of
hair and geometrically printed cape. Her legs were OK and
her feet looked good in little suede boots. She went in and
out in the traditional places as far as Bill could tell. But that
wasn't far. When would those designer wimps stop trying
to square the circle and circle the square?

'Well?' Baxter repeated. He was behind his desk now,
surveying her above the rim of his paper coffee-cup. She
took a seat opposite. With the gestures of a classy striptease
artist she unpeeled her gloves and unbuttoned her cape, to
reveal a matching dress. He looked away from the cutaway
triangle of flesh between her breasts.

'You've already met Inspector Armstrong.'

'Hi.' Yvonne flashed him a whiter-than-white smile.

Armstrong consulted his notebook. 'You made a statement to Sergeant Short and myself at the Ruffled Feathers
on Friday last. 'Is there anything you wish to add?'

'That's the idea,' she nodded encouragingly. 'I told you
the truth, but not what you might call the whole truth. And
now I've decided to come clean.'

'Why?' Baxter growled.

'It was this.' From her kid pochette she produced a

newspaper cutting. The press release on the Poulencs' death. 'Those poor people.'

'You knew them?'

'Slightly—they were my grandparents' friends. *Grand' maman* was French. She took me and my sister to visit the Poulencs when we were little. I don't think they had a great deal of money, even then. But everything was so elegant. For Lisa and me it was like another world. Mum and Dad are both academics and our house was always strewn with books and papers. At the Poulencs our orange juice came in cut glass tumblers, and there were sugared almonds and fondants on paper doilies. And Madame—always so well groomed. It was from her I first learnt to take my appearance seriously. I wept when I read about those plastic bags. Can you believe me, Chief Inspector?' She leant forward, her grey eyes luminous, the shadow deepening between her breasts. Baxter nodded.

Too bloody right, he could. Armstrong vented his scorn on a marginal doodle. Nice girls and tarts still came separately packaged, as far as he was concerned. But the old man dreamed sweeter dreams.

'I mustn't waste your time,' Yvonne was murmuring.

'About Thursday night . . .'

'Yes, I don't suppose there's any connection. But I thought . . . just in case. Murder's a serious business, isn't it?'

'The most serious, in my book.'

'That Hobbs woman, the Poulencs. There might be others. People of my own age.'

'Or younger. Thursday evening?'

'I was bored. Bored out of my little mind. Worst of it was, they seemed to be having a good time in the brasserie. I'd have liked to go in there. But I'd promised Ted.'

'The boss?'

'The husband.'

'How long did you stick it?'

'Till around 9.55. Then I got this yen for a cigarette. So I asked Dr Denny if he'd like his bill. Not the done thing to rush them, but I didn't think he'd make a fuss. Anyhow, he paid up straight away, and after I'd brought back his change I slipped out again. First to the Ladies and then to my locker in the passage to get a ciggy. Ted doesn't like the smell, but if I smoke in the open air it doesn't cling the same. So I went out by the staff entrance and round the corner into the main restaurant car park. I knew it would be empty, except for Dr Denny's car.'

'There's a separate park for the restaurant customers?'

'A small one—most customers don't know about it. It's out of sight of the brasserie and the main road.'

'How long did you stay there?'

'Five . . . seven minutes perhaps. I felt much better in the open air. I finished the cigarette and sucked a chlorophyl tablet. Then I heard a car. I drew back round the corner of the building so the headlights wouldn't catch me.'

'What make of car?'

'Silver-blue Porsche convertible. One of the biggies. London registration.'

'Remember the number?'

'God, no. But I was pretty sure I hadn't seen it before. Or the driver. Striking old guy. Shock of grey hair and heavy black eyebrows. Not the sort you'd forget in a hurry.'

'Did you go back inside?'

'I was going to when the restaurant door opened and Dr Denny came out.'

'How did he seem?'

'Uptight, I thought. Hesitated, and looked all round him. Then he walked over to the Porsche, very fast, and got into the passenger's seat.'

'What did you do then?'

'Went back inside, cleared up in the restaurant, sat around. Ten-thirty the boss looked in. Saw there were no customers and said I could pack it in.'

'And Dr Denny?'

'Still in the Porsche last thing before I left. Had to go over to the windows of the restaurant to check the catches.'

'Could you see how he looked?'

'Not really. It was raining cats and dogs by then. You could just see vague blobs of faces and shirtfronts. Oh, and the glint of something. Wedding-ring, perhaps. Denny seemed to be stuffing something into his pocket.'

'It's highly inconvenient, Chief Inspector.' The lines at the side of Eileen Lethbridge's mouth tensed disapprovingly. 'Case conference afternoon. Whole team is involved.'

'Murder is inconvenient, Mrs Lethbridge.'

'Yes, well, if you put it like that, I suppose . . .' She sighed, pressing a key on the intercom. For several seconds the two detectives waited, contemplating the neat desk and behind it the filing-cabinet in which Cheryl Hobbs had found her last reading matter. The alphabetic range of the contents of each drawer was indicated in elegant gothic script.

'Are you a student of calligraphy, Mrs Lethbridge?' Baxter asked, and watched the flush of unexpected pleasure spread below the film of rouge and down her neck.

'One of my hobbies. You may go in now. They're all next door. In the Medical Director's office.'

'Sorry to interrupt,' Baxter began.

'Are you really, Chief Inspector?' Hilde Tomlinson mocked.

'Hilde, please . . .'

'Sorry, Peter. It's just that the social lies seem more than usually inappropriate.'

'I'm inclined to agree, Mrs Tomlinson. And I'm sure that you and your colleagues won't take it amiss if I say we should like to see Dr Denny alone in the first instance.'

'Very well.' Hilde made something of a business of assembling her papers. 'We'll see you later, Peter. Not too much later, I trust. Meantime we'll do what we can without you. Mrs Gordon, Mr Aiken and I will be in my office, Chief Inspector. No doubt you'll let us know if and when you require us.'

'Thank you.' As he held the door open for her, Baxter conceded that Hilde could look good if she tried. And she hadn't given up trying. Her violet wool dress clung to her firm breasts and bypassed her thick waist. Her upswept hair gave the illusion of above average height.

'Well, gentlemen?'

'Well, Dr Denny.' Baxter sat down without invitation and opened his briefcase. 'I should like to know from you who has the second key to your medicine cupboard.'

'No one. It's against regu- . . .'

'Against regulations? Yes. Unless that person is medically or pharmaceutically qualified. But we're not here to bandy statutory orders and instruments, are we? A woman is dead. A child's life is in danger.'

'Oh Christ.' Denny covered his eyes.

'Someone searched that cupboard on Thursday afternoon or evening. If it makes it any easier, I don't believe that person was necessarily the murderer. We think he or she was looking for something. Something that might have proved an embarrassment to you.'

Baxter paused before continuing. 'Can't you give us a name, Dr Denny?'

The psychiatrist raised a stricken face. 'Why drag someone else into the dirt?'

'You wouldn't be doing that. But if you refuse to cooperate, you'll force our hand.'

Denny sighed. 'Very well. It was probably Hilde. She had the key copied long ago . . . I suppose she may still have it.'

'What would she have been looking for? Methadone?'

'It seems light years ago—fifteen, I suppose. We ran an

evening clinic for young drug addicts. Not here . . . on the other side of town. Hilde and I, plus a couple of part-time nurses. We used counselling mainly, but I prescribed methadone for a few cases. People thought it was a good idea in those days. Part of the weaning process.'

'Go on.'

'It was tough work. Too tough for me, with all the other projects we had on hand and my marriage hitting its first low. Hilde was marvellous. So committed, so strong. I felt I must keep it going for her sake. Couldn't bear to let her down. His voice broke.

'So you began to inject?'

'Once or twice a week at first. Then every day. But not for long. Three or four weeks perhaps. Then one of my patients caught me at it. No names, no packdrill, poor bastard. Tried to blackmail me.'

'Only tried?'

'I'd the sense to see it was only his word against mine, and he'd a record behind him. I did what I should have done when things got on top of me—talked to Hilde. We backed out of the undertaking—said we'd too many other irons in the fire, which was true enough, God knows. And she bullied me into seeking treatment from the best man in the business. Three months and I was cured.'

'But Mrs Tomlinson kept an eye on you?'

'Yes. She had the key cut and she made regular inspections. Finally, several years later, we were both convinced I'd never relapse. The subject was dropped between us.'

'Till Cheryl Hobbs raised it last March?'

'Yes. Hilde told me she'd lied to you to protect me. To protect human resources therapy too, she said. I've been going through hell about it, but she persuaded me that it would be self-indulgent to come clean.'

'Any idea how Cheryl could have picked up the story?'

'We assumed she'd heard it at the Foxwillow Arms when

she worked there. It was closed down after a drugs scandal. My ex-patient probably picked up some of his supplies there —may even have become a pusher.'

'Must have been unnerving, this emergence of the old skeleton?'

'Horrific. If Mrs Hobbs had decided to blackmail me, she'd probably have made a good job of it. Might even have put Martin up to lying. Therapy's a risky business at the best of times.'

'But she didn't?'

'No, thank God.' It was touching, that quick, boyish smile in the worn face. Baxter could imagine its appeal to a protective woman, a close colleague. 'I assume she'd better things to do. Decided the game wasn't worth the candle.'

'Must have been worrying, all the same. Especially as you were subjected to other stresses.'

'I don't know . . .'

'London job folding, for instance. That was bugging you badly last Thursday, wasn't it? So you contacted your old specialist, didn't you? But he couldn't see you in Town. Why not?'

'He was dining out, if you must know. Somewhere in Herts.'

'So he offered to meet you afterwards at the Ruffled Feathers?'

'This has nothing to do with . . .'

'Hasn't it? Doing pretty well, isn't he, Dr Whatshisname? Driving a snazzy new Porsche, we hear. And he brought a little something to cheer you up, didn't he? What was it, Dr Denny?'

'The mixture as before, Chief Inspector. The hearing ear. Sympathy. Realism. The man doesn't use medication.'

'We'll need to know his name,' Baxter continued, gentle now. 'Especially as you were seen to put something in your pocket.'

'Pock . . . Oh, I daresay it was one of these!' Denny produced a monogrammed handkerchief. 'Tissues are one of my wife's pet hates.'

'The name,' Baxter repeated quickly, to cover his embarrassment. 'We've a fair description, and it shouldn't take the lads long to work through the possibles. But they've better things to do with their time, don't you think?'

'Of course.' Denny removed a card from his wallet and passed it across the desk.

'Tell me, Dr Denny. Did Martin Hobbs ever indicate that he believed you to be his father?'

'If you've read the casenotes, you'll already know the answer. If you know anything of psychoanalytic theory you'll have heard of the patient's transference of feelings for the parent on to the therapist. A well-established phenomenon, in my experience.'

'Did it go further in Martin's case than in most?'

'At times. Like many kids deprived of normal family relationships, Martin compensated through what has been called the Cinderella complex. He glamorized the absent parent—rejected the unexciting reality. In Martin's case his mother's tendency to devalue her ex-husband fed the delusion. But he was intelligent enough to know he was deceiving himself.'

'I wonder. He must have felt himself to be on solid ground to have confided in his school friend. Perhaps he saw or heard something recently to confirm his theory.'

'Perhaps.'

'Mrs Hobbs was an attractive, ambitious woman, in search of a husband. If she knew of your past involvement with drugs, Dr Denny, she may have known other personal details . . . such as the state of your marriage.'

'Possibly.' Denny spoke in the flat tones of the chronically depressed.

'Are you sure that Thursday was the first evening this year that Mrs Hobbs visited the clinic? Did you not invite

her to meet you last spring to discuss the drugs business?
Did she not propose marriage as the price of her silence?
Did you not meet her on several later occasions, including
last Thursday afternoon?'

'No.' He spoke without conviction, almost as if he wished
to be doubted.

'Very well, Dr Denny. An unpleasant duty.'

'In the words of my old housemaster.' The Medical
Director managed a smile.

As Baxter rose to go, he was disturbed by the words and
the glimmerings of sadism which had been ignited in him
by his informant's passivity.

'Shan't detain you for long,' the Chief Inspector assured
Hilde Tomlinson as he closed the door behind her departing
colleagues. 'I've brought back your book.'

'Well, what's the verdict?' She raised her brown eyes.

'I'm hardly qualified to judge, but . . .'

'But . . .' The hesitation seemed to amuse her.

'It read like a defence of professionalism.'

She laughed. 'Sit down, Mr Baxter. I think we understand
one another. Not that you are being altogether fair, of course.
All the same, there's more than a grain of truth in your
assessment. The buck could and should be tossed around
rather more freely than it is in child guidance, but in the
long run, as you know and I know, it's going to be dumped
on the experts.'

'Yes, I rather suspect that we share one thing, you and
I. An over-developed sense of responsibility.'

Hilde's smile faded. 'Is that why you came in here alone?'

'Partly. Dr Denny has told me about his drug problem.'

'I see.'

'And about Cheryl Hobbs's accusation. Are you prepared
to come down to the station later on to amend your statement?'

'Certainly. I didn't lie for the sake of lying. Peter needed time . . . I wasn't just being sentimental, you know. He's a brilliant diagnostician. And with suitable clients, a fine therapist . . .'

He let her weep for several minutes before speaking.

She wiped her eyes. 'Forgive me if I embarrassed you. I don't often . . . I hope none of this methadone thing need come out.'

'I can't promise. We must consider the child.'

'I should have thought he was physically safe as long as he was in care. Unless the murderer is a psychopath. And psychopaths are thin on the ground, aren't they?'

'Yes, thank God.'

'Any more questions, Chief Inspector? If not . . .'

'You would like to resume your conference, I expect. Let's go down together.'

There was a sudden silence when the social worker opened Peter Denny's door.

'One last thing before we leave you in peace.' Baxter addressed himself to the psychiatrist. 'It occurred to me earlier this afternoon that Cheryl Hobbs may not have confined her attentions to Martin's file. That she may not even have been killed for reading Martin's file.'

'But surely . . .' Jane Gordon protested.

'Do you mind if we make a physical inspection of the file covers in the E to K drawer? We shall, of course, consult with you should examination of the contents of any of them seem to be indicated.'

'Well . . .' Peter Denny's eyes interrogated Hilde's.

'Mrs Lethbridge will keep us in good order.'

'You can bet your life on that, Peter,' Jos Aiken boomed.

'For what it's worth. Very well, Chief Inspector. Do what you must.'

CHAPTER 13

It was four am. Martin sat on the bank at one end of the layby, watching the parked lorry and waiting. He was good at waiting. Besides, he was tired. He had slept from nine to three last night but very little during his first three nights at Whitelands. There was no frost but it was too chilly to sit outdoors in total comfort. He drew up the hood of his anorak and pulled mittens over chafed palms. Luckily his skinned knees were hidden and there were no other visible signs of his descent by drainpipe. He inspected the contents of his haversack to find they had survived his stumbles on the poorly maintained right-of-way across fields from a minor road to the A11.

Half an hour later the door of the lorry opened. The registration plate bore a Belgian code, but the driver, a tall, swarthy man, looked Italian. Spoil children rotten, those Italians, his mother used to say. Martin drew a deep breath, waiting unnoticed until the man had peed, returned to his cab and switched on the radio. Then he walked out in front of the vehicle, shouting and gesticulating. The driver opened his window, yawned and beckoned.

'Where?'

'Cambridge—Addenbrooke's Hospital.

'You sick?'

'My father. I'm going to see my father.'

'Middle of the night?'

'He's very sick. There was a 'phone call. My aunt said I could go by the first bus but that's not till nine. Might be too late. Haemorrhage, they said.' He was surprised that the tears came so quickly and naturally.

'*Quanto* . . . how old?'

'Fifteen.'

'She knows where you are, this aunt?'

'I left a note.'

The driver opened the passenger door.

'Let's see what you got in the bag.'

Martin handed up the haversack, watching hairy hands unbuckle the straps. The driver opened the pencil box, sniffed at the Indian ink, inspected the drawings.

'*Uccelli* . . . You study birds?'

'Dad knows about them. He taught me.' How easy it was, when you got going, this mixing of fact and makebelieve. Like remaking your world.

The driver jerked his head. 'Come. It's against the rule, but come.'

Martin climbed up beside him and accepted a mugful of hot, bitter coffee.

At 4.30 Baxter was drifting into his last sleep of a restless night. A night haunted by the recurring image of the blood-flecked but uninformative sheet of A4 they had found in Louise Henderson's file. And by the nasal twang of Armstrong's voice as they left the clinic the previous afternoon.

'What are we waiting for?'

'Lab report for one thing.' And for a face, a face he was struggling to disentangle from his memories of the photographs in the Hendersons' breakfast-room.

'Risky. Someone's bound to talk.' He jerked his head.

'The professionals? Shouldn't think so. Stakes are too high now on the survival of their little empire. And Eileen doesn't know which file we took.' With Denny's permission they had left the cabinet locked and sealed and removed both sets of keys.

'What about the kid? He'll be out of shock by now. Might have remembered something. Shouldn't we . . .?'

'It'll keep.'

But would it? Baxter dreamt in his last morning sleep

that he was lying under a motheaten tigerskin like one on his grandfather's hearth. He imagined now, as then, the creature coming to life, blowing hot breath on his cheeks. flexing its claws on his shoulders. He lay paralysed, listening to the snufflings, anticipating the first deep stabs. The telephone had rung for several seconds before he accepted the fact of his release.

Sarah, flushed and tousled, handed him the receiver. Colin Short was speaking from the incidents room.

'Lad's absconded.'

'Bloody hell.' It was a home with a good record. Social Services had sworn they'd keep a close but unobtrusive eye on the boy.

'When?'

'Some time after two. Another kid saw him in bed then.'

Seven-fifty by Baxter's watch. No point in a dash to Norfolk at this late stage. Chances were that the boy had slipped out before daybreak. Could be anywhere by now.

'Notify all police authorities in the region. Hold the media statement.'

'Place of bloody safety,' he grumbled to Armstrong ten minutes later. They were breakfasting in his office off weak Nescafé and tough croissants. Armstrong listened on an extension 'phone as he received the warden's report of an unlocked landing window and the duty worker's four am visit to the lavatory.

'Why?' Homesickness, the warden supposed. Boy hadn't opened up to his staff. Hardly surprising. You couldn't rush things with this sort of trauma. He'd conformed, settled into their routine. They hadn't sent him to school yet but they'd organized morning lessons with a peripatetic teacher in a group for disturbed children. They'd taken him out and about with this bunch in the afternoons. He'd done some sketches of birds in the grounds and gone shopping with a housemother to buy drawing materials. Money? He might have two or three pounds on him. Broke into a fiver the day he went shopping.

Precipitating factors? Nothing the warden could put a finger on. The aunt had rung a couple of times but Martin hadn't shown any strong reaction. She was coming to visit at the weekend. Father had rung yesterday but he wasn't allowed to speak to the boy. Housemother had simply told him his father would like to visit sometime. Asked him how he felt about the idea. Martin had seemed a bit shaken, so she'd made a point of assuring him that he needn't see Hobbs yet if he didn't want to. He had seemed to accept the assurance, but there was no way of knowing. So many of the kids who came to Whitelands had forgotten the meaning of the word 'trust'—or never learnt it.

'He's wrong, isn't he?' Baxter observed when he'd rung off. 'Martin Hobbs trusts at least one person.'

'His aunt?'

'I was thinking of the man he has cast in the role of his father.' He wiped his face on a paper napkin. 'But we'd better look in on Freda all the same before we alert the media.'

Freda's narrow eyes condemned him above her half-lenses. She jabbed rhythmically at a multicoloured garment of uncertain purpose.

'Martin would have been better off here. Safe at least.'

'I doubt that,' the Chief Inspector objected. 'Unless you'd kept him under lock and key. He was better off out of Holtchester.'

'But he's running back, isn't he?'

'How can you be so certain?'

'Martin's insecure. Always was. Oh, he improved out of all recognition after he went to Browne. But he's not the adventurous type. I'm surprised he plucked up courage for this move. He didn't sound too bad when I spoke to him on the 'phone yesterday. But I suppose he was lonely. Or frightened.'

'Steve Hobbs rang Whitelands yesterday as well. Wanting to visit.'

'Oh, no.' Freda's hand flew to her mouth. 'He promised.' She closed her eyes for a good minute, head bowed, knitting discarded in her lap. Baxter made silencing gestures in the direction of his embarrassed colleague.

'There's something I should have told you earlier, but I didn't . . . didn't want to give the wrong impression about Steve.' She bit her lower lip. 'But now I know I must tell you. It's the Lord's will.'

'Go on.'

'It was about six weeks ago—late on a Sunday evening. Cheryl had been up in London as usual and had called round here to collect Martin. The heating had broken down on the train and she seemed chilled, so I asked her in for a cup of tea. She couldn't have been in the house for more than a couple of minutes when the bell rang again. It was Steve, asking to see Cheryl. I'd told him about her remarriage plans only the Monday before. He'd obviously been drinking and he looked flushed and angry. I've never seen him in such a state before or since. He pushed past me and headed for this room, where the light was on. He shouted to Martin to go upstairs and I offered to go too, but Cheryl begged me to stay. I could see she was terrified.

'He kept himself under control to begin with. I persuaded them both to sit down and keep their voices low for the child's sake. He congratulated Cheryl, asked for the name and address of the prospective husband. Cheryl kept cool too. Said he'd have the information in good time. The wedding wouldn't take place for some months yet. And there were reasons, professional reasons, why she couldn't name names yet.

'"Professional!" Steve shouted at her. He was really worked up now. "That's a good one. I dare say there are so many names you get them mixed up once in a while."

'"Shut up!" Cheryl shouted back.

'"Shut up yourself, you little whore!

'I stood there, praying for the Lord to put the right words into my mouth. Maybe I didn't pray hard enough. Maybe I wanted Cheryl to get hurt. Anyway, very soon after that I heard the banister creak and knew that Martin had been up there, listening. Steve must have heard it too. He stood up, grey in the face, holding on to the arm of the settee.

'"Just get this straight, Cheryl," he said. "I've gone easy on access for the boy's sake, not yours. But if you and your mystery man think you can outsmart me, you've got a big shock coming. Any dirty tricks and I'll take action. Appropriate action."

'Then he slammed out of the house. When Martin came downstairs he ran straight to his mother. I just stood there like a fool, saying nothing that made sense. I'm sure Steve was referring to legal action, but Martin mightn't have known that. Last Thursday evening he could very well have put two and two together and made five. Suspected his father of murdering his mother.'

'Hobbs boxed the poor kid in, didn't he? You don't think Martin's going for him?'

'Not single-handed. All the same . . .' She shivered.

Baxter dictated the media release over the police car radio and asked Short to contact Hobbs via the bus depot. At a quarter to nine they were outside the Forbes' house.

Susie opened the door, already dressed in her outdoor clothes. Hearing the voices, her mother emerged from the kitchen.

'You said not to push her.'

'That's right. But something's happened. Martin's made off from the children's home. I imagine he's running back to his friends, but he could be running into danger.'

'Dear God.' Vera Forbes wiped detergent foam off her thin fingers.

'So you must let us know right away if he contacts you, Susie. Promise?'

She nodded dumbly.

'He'll go somewhere he feels safe. Probably to this man he says is his father. I know you gave him your word, but things are different now. I need to have the name.'

'Hendy . . . Mr Henderson,' she mumbled.

'He couldn't possibly . . .' Vera Forbes cried out, then subsided. 'The Hendersons were living miles away when Martin was born.'

'I know,' Baxter said gently. 'I'd say Martin knows, deep down,' he added, remembering the torn-up photographs. 'Thanks for telling us, Susie. You'll let us know if you hear anything?' He scribbled down the number of the incident room.

'All right.' She buttoned the hood of her navy jacket, stiffening beneath her mother's consolatory hug.

'London? Where?' The Chief Inspector could hear the panicky squeak in his voice and knew that the school secretary heard it too.

'The Department of Education—Elizabeth House.' He cursed himself silently, remembering the felt tip entry on John Henderson's year organizer and his assumption that they referred to the headquarters of some local institution.

'When does the meeting begin?'

Viv Wallace's waved head bent over the desk diary. 'Eleven. But Mr Henderson said he'd probably take an early train. He'd a report to pick up from the Government Bookshop, I understand.'

'Drives a Toyota, doesn't he?'

'No . . . yes, of course. Stupid of me. Mr Henderson took delivery of the car at the beginning of the month.'

'And the last one? What model did he drive before this?'

'A Maestro . . . a red Maestro. But why . . . you surely don't . . .' Her face surrendered briefly to fear.

'Did he leave a 'phone number . . . an extension?'

'Oh, yes.' She copied it out for him. 'Mr Henderson's punctilious about leaving a number when he's on duty.'

'On duty? It's a full-time job, isn't it?'

'Job and a half, we tell him.' She managed a smile. 'On top of his regular school commitments, he still gives a lot of time to the youth club and weekend community events. So he takes two afternoons as token time off in lieu. Spends them in the open air if possible.'

'Which two afternoons?'

'Mondays and Thursdays.'

'We're making the incidents room feel they're needed, if we're doing nothing else,' Baxter commented after his next brief radio conference. His companion recognized a conscious attempt to reduce the heightened blood pressure which could interfere with crisis management. The news from the station that Steve Hobbs had reported sick after an hour on duty that morning had hit the Chief Inspector hard. The conviction was growing in him that the bus driver was holding back on something more significant than his meeting in Freda Taylor's house with his ex-wife.

Baxter rang the bell of the Henderson villa. No reply. He rang again. Two bottles of milk stood on the doorstep. The lined curtains of the front bedroom were drawn. Armstrong walked round the house and noted the remains of breakfast for one on a kitchen table.

'Can I help?' A tall redhead looked over the garden fence. 'Can I take a message?'

'No thanks. I imagine Mrs Henderson is having a lie-in.'

'I suppose so. Not a bit like Louise, though. She's a born lark. I do hope nothing's wrong.'

'No reason why there should be. We'll be back later. In the meantime, if you see anything to worry you . . .' He handed over a card.

'I don't like it,' Armstrong muttered, as they retreated to the car.

'Do you think for one bloody minute that I do?' his senior snapped, switching on the transceiver to learn that Henderson's car was parked at Cambridge station. It looked as if the Acting Head had taken one of the early morning expresses or had wished to give that impression.

'Still nothing firm on the boy?' Baxter asked Short on their return to Headquarters.

'Half a dozen calls but mostly unconvincing. Best lead's from a taxi driver who saw a kid fitting his description cycling down Station Road, Cambridge, around 5.30.'

'Station bloody Road!'

'Have I said something?'

'No . . . I don't know . . . go on.'

'That's it, except this kid was wobbling about. Saddle on the high side. Bike could have been stolen.'

It was a quarter to ten when Martin rode off the highway into the lane leading to Chess Wood. The road was quiet now, but the rush hour had been in full spate when he had ridden out of Cambridge, inconspicuous among the hundreds of young cyclists. He had dyed his hair with the Indian ink in the cold hours spent in back alleys waiting for the shops to open. And he had discarded his anorak in favour of a newly acquired secondhand duffel coat. He knew full well that they would be searching for him, but he had no fear of being caught. He felt a different person since he had spoken to his father.

He hid the bicycle in the hawthorn hedge that bounded the ancient wood, and walked up the lane. As he drew near the trees he could hear the hiss of the wind in their leaves.

Snakes, he had told Susie last summer. Cobras ready to pounce. They had laughed then, frightening themselves silly and enjoying every minute of it. He wouldn't think of snakes today. He couldn't afford to be frightened with six more hours to put in on his own. Four-thirty, his father had said. He turned off the lane and down a ride of beech trees. This year's leaves were almost ready to fall, but you'd never guess it from looking. They were too perfect, too golden. Last autumn's fall lay beautifully preserved, a ceremonial carpet.

He walked the quarter mile to the Outdoor Pursuits Centre, a converted and extended shooting lodge. The official wording on the plaque commemorating its opening gave him pause. He felt for a moment the old panic, the old urge to run home. But there was no home to run to. Not yet. His father had told him to wait at his aunt's house until it was time for their meeting. But he knew better. Freda meant well but she wasn't to be trusted. Nor her God either. *Oh God our help in ages past* he'd sung beside her in chapel. But he'd stopped believing it years ago. 'Learn to fight your own corner,' his mother had said. 'No one else will do it for you.' He was learning. With his Dad to back him, he'd fight hers as well.

He went round to the back of the building, took off his duffel coat and wrapped it round his right fist. With eyes closed, he punched the pantry window as hard as he knew how.

At eleven-fifteen Baxter made his second telephone call to the Department of Education and Science. The meeting was in progress but there was as yet no sign of Henderson and no message.

'Hell.'

'Reckon it was a blind?' Armstrong asked.

'Probably. In any event, we'd better pull the stops out. Try to check whether he made it to Liverpool Street.'

'We'll need help.'

'Of course.'

'And permission from the CC?'

' 'Fraid so.' The Chief Inspector grimaced as he keyed in the familiar code.

'You've lost the boy and you've lost your chief suspect. Messy business.' Montgomery's sibilants insulted the ear.

'Looks that way, sir. That's why we need extra resources.'

'Pricey business, too.'

'Maybe. But as you've said yourself on more than one occasion, it pays to spend at the right time.'

'And today's the right time? Not yesterday, for instance?'

'We must hope not, sir.'

'Very well then. But you'd bloody well better prove it.'

'Good thing he doesn't know we've lost Hobbs as well,' Armstrong murmured in the douce tones of bourgeois Ulster.

'Hobbs is all right,' Baxter snapped. But was he? For the last couple of hours the Chief Inspector had been discomfited by a scenario which had delayed the call to the Path Lab he now forced himself to make. His face relaxed visibly as he listened.

'Like I said, Hobbs is all right.'

'Why should I believe you?'

'The clearest prints on the Henderson file were made by the person in the tigerskin—the murderer. And one of them was smudged with Cheryl Hobbs's blood.'

'So the murderer was the person who refiled the folder?'

'Uh-huh.'

'An act for which Steve Hobbs could have no obvious motive.'

Baxter laughed. 'Sounds as though we both took an excursion up the same garden path this morning.'

'Even an Ulsterman is capable of original thought once in a while. You don't give me credit . . .'

At twelve they were again standing on the Hendersons'

doorstep. The bedroom windows were open now, but Louise was still in her green towelling dressing-gown when she answered their second ring.

'You were here earlier, my neighbour said. Sorry about that. Took a couple of Dormadon last night. Don't usually, you see, so they knock me out for the count.'

As they followed her past the lounge door there were no longer any *Mikado* costumes in sight. But in the kitchen they could see several packing-cases, partly filled with crockery.

Louise slumped into a chair at the breakfast-room table and the detectives took the places opposite. She sat forward, arms folded beneath her breasts, fingers seeking comfort in the rough warmth of the towelling sleeves. Her dull, puffy face contrasted with its images in the snapshots behind her, which were variously tender, mischievous and anxious, but always very much alive.

'Your husband had planned to go to London this morning, I understand,' the Chief Inspector began.

'Yes.'

'But he hasn't arrived at Elizabeth House.'

'Oh?'

'Any idea where he might be?'

She shook her head. 'I wouldn't. He was leaving me, you see.'

'I'm sorry, but it's important. We need to contact him without delay.'

'I can't help you.' She fumbled for a tissue.

'This leaving business. Was it a sudden decision of your husband's?'

'Not exactly. I was the one who was going away . . . in the literal sense . . . with my kids. He wanted us to stay here but I couldn't bear to. Not when everything was over between us.'

She had found the tissue, but stared at it stupidly, as if forgetting how to use it.

'When did you plan to go?'

'Next week. After the Headship interviews. People are such hypocrites, aren't they? It could have wrecked his chances if we'd split shortly beforehand.'

'But this morning he jumped the gun?'

'Another week. It wasn't much, was it? He might have given me another week.' She stifled her sobs with a clenched fist.

'What made him change his mind?' Baxter asked, smoothing a crumpled cutting his colleague had retrieved from a wastepaper basket.

'He had a phone call about six this morning. It woke me up.'

'Could you hear what was said?'

'No . . . I wasn't altogether with it . . . the pills. Besides, we have separate rooms.' They could see it was a confession of failure. 'But I could hear him moving around soon afterwards. Making himself breakfast. Around seven he came upstairs with a cup of tea.'

'How did he seem?'

'Determined. He had no options left, he said, but to go away. He refused to elaborate. But he was quite relaxed. As though he knew he was doing the right thing. And affectionate. The way he used to be before . . .'

'Before he became involved with her?' Baxter pushed the newspaper cutting across the table. It was a photograph of Cheryl Hobbs, published with the press release on her murder. Someone had scribbled round the hairline in thick black felt-tip.

'You knew?' he asked gently.

'Oh, yes. I fought against it for months, but I knew. The way he looked at her when she came to the house. And when I saw the newspaper photograph I couldn't deceive myself any longer.'

'You can do things to photographs that you can't do to people,' Baxter remarked, studying the scribbles. 'You'd have liked to kill Cheryl Hobbs, wouldn't you?'

She nodded.

'But someone did it for you.'

'I thought things would work out for John and me after she'd gone. I hoped we could live . . . the way we'd always lived. With the twins almost grown up. I'd have more energy to put into the relationship. It wasn't all I wanted, but when I thought of losing him I knew it would be more than enough.'

'But her death made no difference?'

'No.'

'Because Cheryl was a ghost, wasn't she? And you can't kill ghosts.'

She drew in her breath sharply. 'You know . . . I'm glad someone knows.' For a second Baxter grasped the small hand she reached out to him. She wiped her eyes.

'Martin's run away from a children's home. Did you hear that on the radio?'

She shook her head, pale eyes wide in a blotchy face.

'He wouldn't . . . John wouldn't.'

The Chief Inspector stood up. 'I hope you're right, my dear. I very much hope you're right.'

'In a minute.' Baxter sidestepped Steve Hobbs's outstretched arm in the corridor outside the incidents room. 'Taken your time, haven't you? Another minute or two won't hurt.'

'Poor bastard,' said Armstrong.

'Poor me.' His senior rubbed a distended abdomen. 'Get someone to lay on rolls and soup in my office, will you?'

He took comfort from the commuters' reports that John Henderson's journey on the 8.40 had continued as far as London. Martin's pick-up driver hadn't yet come forward, but a Cambridge charity shop worker had remembered selling a duffel coat to a boy with badly dyed hair and an appearance that otherwise fitted Martin's shortly after nine. Half an hour later a duffel-coated boy cyclist had been seen leaving the city by the Huntingdon Road.

'Huntingdon? Why Huntingdon?' Armstrong had asked with obsessive insistence.

'Why not? He's a bright lad. Had to take one detour or another if he wanted to hold us off. Probably lying low till dark.

'Fancy some nosh?' The Chief Inspector gestured to the plastic trays awaiting him in his office.

Hobbs shook his head. 'Freda heated up a pie for me but I couldn't face it.'

'Did she tell you what she told us?'

'Sorry. It didn't seem important, you see. I'd just lost the head—Cheryl realized . . .'

'But Martin didn't.'

'No, God forgive me. It didn't dawn on me that he'd heard—Freda was wrong there.' The flabby face contorted. 'Must have come back to him afterwards. He must be sure I killed his Mum. Hard to take, that, after all I did to play him along gently.'

Baxter belched. 'Is that why you came over here?'

'No.'

'Get on with it then.'

'I heard the lunchtime news at Freda's. You're looking for Henderson. I thought I'd better tell you he's the man Cheryl was going to marry.'

'How long have you known?'

'Not until the week before she died.'

'Why the hell didn't you tell us sooner?'

'What good would that have done? Henderson isn't a bad man, by all accounts. If Cheryl was having it off with that social worker fellow under his nose she deserved everything she got. Martin hadn't guessed as far as I knew, and he'd been through enough without that. Why should I bring his world crashing round his ears?'

'Not if it could prove your innocence?'

Hobbs shook his head. 'He'd never forgive me. Henderson's his big hero. You can't love to order. If I've learnt one thing in this world it's that.'

'Where did he take her?'

'To Chess Wood. Anyway, that's where they went the day I followed them. There are several entrances. I thought I knew the place but that afternoon they took a couple of B roads and ended up at a rusty little gate I'd never noticed before. I had to drive a good quarter mile further to get out of sight of his car. It was cold but dry, and I had to keep my distance in the wood. The leaves made one helluva noise underfoot. By the time I got within sight of the central clearing they were twenty minutes ahead of me. I took cover in some hazel bushes and waited. It was a good hour before the lodge door opened and out they came. They started to fool round like a couple of kids. He was lifting up handfuls of leaves and throwing them at her. She was laughing and egging him on. He's in good shape, that chap, a far cry from those weedy types she'd been playing about with in the bookshop. You could see that he really might turn her on. And she . . . it was the first time in my life I noticed it . . . she could almost have been a boy, the way she ran, with her hair pushed up under her cap.'

'Thank you, Mr Hobbs,' Baxter extended his hand. 'Sorry if I was on the sharp side. It's been a difficult day.'

The bus driver rose awkwardly. 'Find him. Tell him whatever you like about me. It doesn't matter. I swear to God I'll never lean on him again. Charge me for obstruction —anything. But find him.'

'We'll try. Now perhaps you'll give us a chance to get on . . .'

The telephone rang before the office door closed on Hobbs. Armstrong pounced on it.

'Report from the Met. Henderson hired a Maxi from the City branch of London Crosscountry Car Rentals shortly before ten this morning.'

*

Martin turned his face away from the sun and into the pillow. The bunk mattress was hard, the blankets prickly and slightly damp. But he had slept longer than he had slept at a stretch in Norfolk, and dreamt comforting dreams. If he lay there a little longer he could store those dreams, hoard them like emergency rations for the remaining hours he must spend alone. He put his arms up and hugged the pillow as he had hugged his mother first thing every morning, when she lay warm and sleepy, washed clean of her usual perfume and smelling faintly of last night's after-shower talc.

Ten minutes later, he felt the beginnings of cramp. He knew from his gym training how easy it was to stiffen up. And he couldn't afford to be unfit today. Rousing himself, he got out of bed and walked over to the window, shivering. The beeches stood brilliant and inviting against a blue sky. He'd never seen this view before, never been inside the male staff bedroom. The boys' dormitory had been locked today. And this room, with its wildlife posters and rag rugs, had a cosier atmosphere. He was cheered by the First Aid box and rows of paperbacks on John Henderson's shelves. He'd find himself something to read when he came back from his walk. From ingrained habit he paused to straighten up the bed. As he lifted the underblanket he saw something glint between headrails and mattress. With difficulty he released the mattress from the metal frame, and groped beneath it.

There was no mistaking them—the earrings in the shape of oak leaves he had given his mother last summer. He sniffed the pillow again, inhaling her talc and the smell of her body. Why should he be surprised, he asked himself. Where else should his mother have lain but in his father's bed? When he had told John Henderson on the 'phone that morning that he knew everything, Hendy must have assumed he knew this as well. When he showed him the earrings there would be no further need for explanations. Overwhelmed by an emotion he could only partly understand, he stuffed the bronze leaves into one of the side pockets of his jeans.

He was glad of the duffel coat when he stepped outside, conscious of a need, not yet urgent, to urinate. A keen wind blew now, hissing loudly through the trees. Traffic rumbled reassuringly on the road below and he had a momentary impulse to head in its direction. Instead he forced himself to take the walk he had enjoyed most in the summer. The birdboxes they used to inspect daily were empty, but crows were cawing overhead. A grey squirrel scuttled up a tree-trunk within a yard of him. The path led through a clearing where sawn-off logs had been left as a habitat for insects. They were in hiding now, those tiny foragers whose purposeful scuttlings he and his classmates had filmed and analysed under Hendy's guidance.

As he walked on, eyes down, an unfamiliar creaking noise brought him to a standstill. Looking up, he caught a glimpse of black and yellow stripes some ten yards ahead. For half a second he froze. Then he moved forward without fear, without any emotion, to confront his nightmare. As he drew close, the figure in the tiger skin swayed above him. His eyes travelled downwards from the bowed hooded head to the freckled wrists above the bloodied mitts. The pale flesh gleamed against darkening veins.

He ran then, faster than he had ever run, from the sight of this unlooked-for death towards the sound of life. But it was not many minutes before his nightmare overtook him. Stumbling over a hidden root, he fell, abandoning himself to the last comforter of rejected creatures, sobbing and peeing into the cold earth.

CHAPTER 14

'It was good of you to tell me yourself. Good of you to come alone.' Louise Henderson had made her own efforts for an expected guest, dressing in a brown worsted frock of severe design and receiving him in the relative formality of her lounge.

'You knew, didn't you?' Baxter's gaze switched briefly from the troubled eyes. The bronze comb and Indian shawl which enlivened her sombre outfit had been placed with the art that conceals art.

'I guessed.'

'Who was he?' Baxter picked up the silver-framed photograph from the side table. The boy had a wide-eyed, pointed face. The face of a sacrificial victim. Cheryl Hobbs's face.

'Guy . . . John's younger brother. There were five years between them . . .'

'You don't have to talk about it.'

'I need to. The parents were missionaries in Malawi— Presbyterian, I think. I've never been into religion. They died there when John was twenty. The boys spent a lot of time together. At their boarding-school and in Cornwall on school holidays. There was a great-aunt there who provided food and accommodation but precious little in the way of interest or affection, as far as I could make out. The boys were very close. They were both keen on sports, especially swimming. Their father encouraged it when he visited. By all accounts he was one of those muscular Christian types.'

Louise produced a photograph album from a wall-cupboard. Baxter flicked through the pages. Facially dissimilar, the brothers had the same broad-shouldered, narrow-hipped physique. And they confronted the camera with the same easy grace. No doubt but they had been leaders of their teenage packs.

'Guy was fifteen when his parents died,' Louise went on. 'It was all very sudden—gastroenteritis. There was a scholarship to cover his school fees but not much else. John felt terribly responsible—thought he shouldn't marry until Guy had settled down. That took quite some time. Guy scraped into London University but failed his First Year BA exams. Didn't bother about the resits. After that he just bummed around for three or four years. Took a few dead-end jobs—travel courier, that sort of thing. When he got into money jams, old John would be on hand to help him out. Finally, in his mid-twenties he seemed to pull himself together. Got a job as a swimming-coach. He'd stuck it out for a year when John and I got married.'

She went over to the drinks cupboard.

'What will you have?' she asked, pouring herself a tonic water.

'Same as you.'

She resettled herself on the sofa, leaning forward now, caressing the tumbler with faintly trembling hands.

'We'd been married about six months when Guy was killed. Road accident—his mini crashed into the back of a bus. Drunken driving—the usual thing. His passenger died too. A young actor about his own age. When John went to Guy's flat to sort things out he discovered that this boy had been Guy's lover. And it was obvious from letters that he hadn't by any means been the first.

'John was devastated. It took me weeks to worm the facts out of him. And when he expressed his reaction, it was in terms of failing in his duty to Guy and to his parents. He was frightfully puritanical at the time as regards deviance of any kind. Just couldn't admit to the jealousy that was screwing him up. Not that there had been anything overtly sexual between him and Guy—I feel sure of that.'

'No.' Cheryl's body had shown no trace of sodomy.

'I almost wish there had. The rejection would have been less . . . less personal. Anyhow, our sex life took a rapid downwards plunge. I gave him time to mourn . . . a whole year. But things didn't change. So I visited a marriage guidance clinic.'

'In Holtchester?'

'No. John was teaching in Fenport then. But, funnily enough, Hilde Tomlinson was working there. The clinic had just been opened and she was helping them out until they had built up their complement of local counsellors.'

'You told me Mrs Tomlinson had been kind to you.'

'She was. But obviously there wasn't much she could do unless John agreed to seek help.'

'And did he?'

'No.' Louise shivered. 'He was furious when he heard what I'd done. Accused me of betrayal, of wanting to drag Guy's name through the mud. I'd no idea he was capable of such anger.'

'So how did you cope?'

'Fought back at first, but that only made matters worse. He clammed up completely. So I cooled down and did my profit-and-loss accounts. John was giving a lot to me and my kids—kindness, security, companionship. And a share in his professional life. It made me good to feel part of the school community. If the other thing had to go—well, I could grin and bear it. For at least as long as the children were dependent. And so it went on. Ten years ago we moved to Holtchester.'

'Ten busy years?'

'Yes.' Louise smiled briefly. 'I hope to God it won't be lost . . . all that graft. I hope they get someone half as good. He *would* have been a good Head, you know.' Her mouth twisted.

'And last July you went to see Mrs Tomlinson again.'

'Did she tell you?'

He shook his head.

'I didn't think so. She was very thoughtful. Gave me an appointment after clinic hours so that I wouldn't run into any of the schoolchildren. Let me into the building herself. Another drink?'

'No, thanks.'

As she drew the curtains and switched on the standard lamp he noticed the smooth lines of her hips and thighs, perceiving for the first time the desirable woman who had not for many years been desired.

'I had to see someone,' she went on, resuming her seat. 'It was the first time it had happened. Then twice in three weeks.'

'What happened?'

She stared past him. 'John called out Guy's name in the night. So loud I could hear him through the dividing wall. Oh, he had wept for him in his sleep often enough. I could take that. But this was different . . . this was a cry of ecstasy. I didn't know what was happening to him and I couldn't bear it. I knew I had to make the break but I needed support.'

'From Mrs Tomlinson?'

'No. After the Fenport business I'd promised John I'd never confide in her again. Besides, it would have been unethical—Mrs T made the point before I could. John's work brought him into professional contact with the Holt-chester clinic.'

'Why did you see her, then?'

'For a referral. She's a big name in social work now, so I assumed she'd know the best people. I didn't tell her any-thing—just said I needed help and asked her to put me in touch with a London counsellor. I go up to visit friends from time to time, so John need never have suspected.' Her voice broke on the word. And for the first time in the interview she covered her face and wept.

'But Mrs Tomlinson made out a file?' Baxter asked softly, when the spasms had subsided.

'Yes . . . she showed me what she'd written. Just the date of the interview and the name of the counsellor she recommended. Said she liked to record all her professional transactions—asked me if I had any objection. I didn't think there was any harm . . . was there? Why are you asking me about it?'

'Because Cheryl Hobbs found the file. Her prints are on it—and the murderer's. He picked up the folder from the desk and refiled it after she died.'

'Oh my God. Do you think that was why . . .?'

'It's not likely.' He didn't want to believe there had been any hesitation, any momentary slackening of the pressure on the carotid artery, as Henderson peered over his victim's shoulder.

'But we can't be sure? He'd want above everything to protect his relationship with Guy—especially from her. And he'd have suspected there was something of substance in my file. It's going to be hard to live with the uncertainty. When did John decide to kill himself?'

'Immediately after the murder—or so he says in this letter to you—here. Sorry it's just a copy. We'll have to keep the original as evidence for the time being. Says he intended to postpone the act until the weekend—half-term. He'd some loose ends of school business to tie up. Wanted to leave a tidy ship for his successor. Martin's 'phone call spoilt that plan. Apparently he just couldn't take the lad's hero-worship.'

There had been no formal written confession—only the symbolic *mea culpa*: the donning of the crumpled disguise Henderson had been carrying in his briefcase. Perhaps his tangled desires never fully emerged into consciousness.

Louise was weeping quietly now, reading the passages of contrition for the damage inflicted on her and her children.

'Will you be all right on your own? Want me to send for someone?'

She shook her head. 'The kids will be home soon. They're

seventeen now . . . stable, sensible kids. We can talk to each other. We'll get by.'

For Martin, Baxter's fears went deeper—and his remorse. As Armstrong drove him to Freda Taylor's house on the pretext of returning the boy's haversack and its contents, he brooded on his failure to avert the confrontation in the woods.

The atmosphere of Freda Taylor's hallway was suffused with spices. From upstairs they could hear muffled bursts of second generation punk.

'How is he?' Baxter asked.

Freda shook her head. 'Who knows? I don't suppose he's begun to take it in. But he wanted to come here. And he says he wants to go back to school after half-term. That's good, the social worker said.'

'Do I smell gingerbread?'

Freda's eyes filled with tears. 'It's silly . . . but I had to do something. He always liked gingerbread. Maybe he'll fancy some. I shan't expect too much—I can guess what it's like for him. There'll be times when he'll hate me for just being alive. I used to feel like that about Cheryl when we were girls, God forgive me. The Lord helped me over it, and He'll help us now. Martin and me.'

'I'm sure He will, Miss Taylor,' said Armstrong. Baxter had a rare pang for the consolations of a religion he did not share, followed by a sense of relief.

'Suppose you're feeling pretty chuffed, Dick?' The Chief Constable's clipped tones crackled over the telephone line.

'Not yet, sir.' Baxter envied his superior's impermeability to the sufferings of the poor, forked creatures whose wounds he salted in the line of duty. But he knew he'd begin to feel better when he had talked to Sarah.

He'd been at it for a good twenty minutes before it was borne in on him that her attention was wavering. She was obviously trying hard to concentrate, but every now and then he'd the sensation that her golden-flecked eyes were looking through him, not at him.

'What's up, love?' He moved across the room to sit beside her.

'Nothing.'

'Come off it.'

'I lost a patient today. Young chap. Postoperative hæmorrhage—it shouldn't have happened. Maybe if I'd pressed for earlier admission . . .'

'Go on. Tell me.'

Listening didn't come any easier for Richard Baxter than it had for Sarah that evening, but he disciplined himself to make the effort. When she had finished, he drew her drained face close and kissed her lightly on the lips.

'We do our best—and it's usually not enough. Feel like some music?'

'Yes, please. Your pick—Mozart?'

She was fond of telling him that the eighteenth century was his spiritual home.

'Too well-mannered. I don't feel well-mannered tonight. Can we have Tippett? The third symphony, for preference.'

'I thought that was your least favourite. Remember how you griped all the way home from that concert in Town? Said you couldn't make head or tail of it.'

'Ah, but I was an uptight bastard in those days, wasn't I?' He drew out the discs from the rack and switched on the player. 'I've come to appreciate the luxury of not having to understand.'

And the luxury of companionship as the music, now scarifying, now consolatory, compelled them to re-enter the forests of twentieth-century night.

If you have enjoyed this book and would like to receive details of other Walker mystery titles, please write to:

Mystery Editor
Walker and Company
720 Fifth Avenue
New York, NY 10019

DATE			